MOONLIGHT
and
FAIRYLAND

MOONLIGHT
and
FAIRYLAND

Laurence Housman

Illustrations by
Pauline Martin

Jonathan Cape
Thirty Bedford Square London

These stories by Laurence Housman first appeared
in *A Farm in Fairyland* 1894; *The House of Joy* 1895;
The Field of Clover 1898; *The Blue Moon* 1904

This selection, first published 1978
under the title of *Moonlight and Fairyland*

© 1978 by Jonathan Cape Ltd
Illustrations © 1978 by Pauline Martin

Jonathan Cape Ltd, 30 Bedford Square, London wc1

British Library Cataloguing in Publication Data

Housman, Laurence
Moonlight and Fairyland.
I. Title
823'.8   pz8
ISBN 0–224–01416–1

Printed in Great Britain
from text composed by Cox & Wyman Ltd
by The Anchor Press Ltd
plates originated and printed by Photo Precision Ltd
bound by Wm Brendon & Son Ltd

Contents

The Traveller's Shoes 7

The Crown's Warranty 26

Japonel 35

The Rooted Lover 42

The Way of the Wind 53

The Moon-flower 69

The Moon-stroke 89

Gammelyn, the Dressmaker 96

White Birch 103

The Luck of the Roses 111

The Prince with the Nine Sorrows 117

List of illustrations with facing page numbers

"There was the red shoe with the pointed toe, cutting capers and prancing about by itself in the middle of the room."   *Page 16*

"Close to her side lay a pair of great shears that shone like blue fire; and while she sang they opened and snapped, keeping time to the music she made."   *Page 20*

"She fetched her crystal ball, and looked in, asking where the king's son might be."   *Page 28*

"'Mother, take off my brother's crown; it pricks me!'"   *Page 32*

"'Why have I not seen that flower before?'"   *Page 48*

"When the dance was over the Prince led her to a seat screened from view by rich hangings of silken tapestry."   *Page 52*

"Katipah went up on to the hill under plum-boughs white with bloom."   *Page 60*

"Catching up Katipah and her child in his arms, he laughed scorn upon those below."   *Page 68*

"Slipping through the window, she stepped out of the Moon, and went running down the same moonbeam by which the pearl had fallen."   *Page 76*

"When he lifted up the earth, out sprang a tiny child like a lobe of quicksilver."   *Page 84*

"'The beautiful is coming true,' thought the Jackdaw, as he yielded to the fairy her wand."   *Page 92*

"He laid the two robes, one on either arm, spreading them abroad till they looked like two wings."   *Page 96*

"Every morning, before it was light, her man and his wife would go into the garden and gather all the roses. Then with full baskets on their backs they would set out."   *Page 112*

"'Drip, drip,' went the roses: wherever she came and kissed, they all began weeping."   *Page 116*

"'Come, come, little peahen, and peck out my heart.'"   *Page 124*

The Traveller's Shoes

LONG while ago there lived a young cobbler named Lubin, who, when his father died, was left with only the shop and the shoe-leather out of which to make his fortune. From morning to night he toiled, making and mending the shoes of the poor village folk; but his earnings were small, and he seemed never able to get more than three days ahead of poverty.

One day, as he sat working at his window-bench, the door opened, and in came a traveller. He had on a pair of long red shoes with pointed ends; but of one the seams had split, so that all his toes were coming out of it.

The stranger, putting up one foot after the other, took off both shoes, and giving that one which wanted cobbling to Lubin, he said: "Tonight I shall be sleeping here at the inn; have this ready in good time tomorrow, for I am in haste to go on!" And having said this he put the other shoe into his pocket, and went out of the door barefoot.

"What a funny fellow," thought Lubin, "not to make the most of one shoe when he has it!" But without stopping to puzzle himself he took up the to-be-mended shoe and set to work. When it was finished he threw it down on the floor behind him, and went on working at his other jobs. He meant to work late, for he had not enough money yet to get himself his Sunday's dinner; so when darkness shut in he lighted a rushlight and cobbled away, thinking to himself all the while of the roast meat that was to be his reward.

It came close on midnight, and he was just putting on the last heel of the last pair of shoes when he was aware of a noise on the floor behind him. He looked round, and there was the red shoe with the pointed toe, cutting capers and prancing about by itself in the middle of the room.

"Peace on earth!" exclaimed Lubin. "I never saw a shoe do a thing so tipsy before!" He went up and passed his hand over it and under it, but there was nothing to account for its caperings; on it went, up and down, toeing and heeling, skipping and sliding, as if for a very wager. Lubin could even tell himself the name of the reel and the tune that it was dancing to, for all that the other foot was missing. Presently the shoe tripped and toppled, falling heel up upon the floor; nor, although Lubin watched it for a full hour, did it ever start upon a fresh jig.

Soon after daybreak, when Lubin had but just opened his shutters and sat himself down to work, in came the traveller, limping upon bare feet, with the shoe's fellow pointing its red toe out of his pocket. "Oh, so," he said, seeing the other shoe ready mended and waiting for him, "how much am I owing you for the job?"

"Just a gold piece," said Lubin, carelessly, carrying on at his work.

"A gold piece for the mere mending of a shoe!" cried the stranger. "You must be either a rogue or a funny fellow."

"Neither!" said Lubin, "and for mending a shoe my charge is only a penny; but for mending *that* shoe, and for all the worry and temptation to make it my own and run off with it—a gold piece!"

"To be sure, you are an honest fellow," said the traveller, "and honesty is a rare gift; though, had you made off with it, I should have soon caught you. Still, you were not so wise as to know that, so here's your gold piece for you." He pulled out a big bag of gold as he spoke, pouring its contents out on to the window bench.

"That is a lot of money for a lonely man to carry about," said Lubin. "Are you not afraid?"

"Why, no," answered the man. "I have a way, so that I can always follow it up even if I lose it." He took two of the gold pieces, and dropped one into the sole of each shoe as he was putting them on. "There!" said he, "now, if any man steal my money, I need only wait till it is midnight; and then I have but to say to my shoes 'Seek!' and up they jump, with me in them, and carry me to where my stolen property is, were it to the world's end. It is as if they had the nose and sagacity of a pair of bloodhounds. Ah, son of a cobbler, had you run off with the one I should have very soon caught you with the other; for if one walks the other is bound to follow. But, as you were honest, we part friends; and I trust God may bring you to fortune." Then the traveller did up his bag of gold, nodded to the cobbler from the doorway, and was gone.

Lubin laid down his work, and went off to the inn. "Did anything happen here last night?" he asked.

"Nothing of much note," answered the inn-keeper. "Three travelling fiddlers were here, and afterwards a man came in barefoot, but with a red shoe sticking out of his pocket. I thought of turning the fellow away, till he let me see the colour of his gold. Presently the fiddlers started to play and the other man to drink. At first when they called on him to dance he excused himself for his feet's sake; but presently, what with the music and the liquor, he got so lively in his head that he pulled on his one shoe and danced like three ordinary men put together."

"What time was that?" asked Lubin.

"Getting on for midnight," answered the inn-keeper.

9

"Ah!" said Lubin, and went home thinking much on the way.

Towards evening he found that he had run out of leather, and must go into the town, ten miles off, to buy more. "Now my gold piece comes in handy," thought he; so he locked up the house, put the key in his pocket, and set out.

Though it was the season of long days it was growing dark when he came to a part of the road that led through the wood; but being so poor a man he had no fear, nor thought at all about the robbers who were said to be in those parts. But as he went, he saw all at once by the side of the road two red spikes sticking up out of a ditch, their bright colour making them plain to the eye. He came quite near and saw that they were two red shoes with pointed toes; and then he saw more clearly that along with them lay the traveller, his wallet empty and with a dagger stuck through his heart.

The cobbler's son was as sorry as he could be. "Alas, poor soul," thought he, "what good are the shoes to you now? Now that thieves have killed you and taken away your gold, surely I do no harm if I give an honest man your shoes!" He stooped down, and was about taking them off when he saw the eyes of the dead man open. The eyes looked at him as if they would remind him of something; and at once, when he loosed hold of the shoes, they seemed satisfied. Then he remembered, and thought to himself, "The world has many marvels in it; I will wait till midnight and see."

For over three hours he kept watch by the dead man's side. "Only last night," he said to himself, "this poor fellow was dancing as merry a measure as ever I saw, for the half of it surely I saw; and now!" Then he judged that midnight must be come, so he bent over the shoes and whispered to them but one word.

The dead man stood up in his shoes and began running.

10

Lubin followed close, keeping an eye on him, for the shoes made no sound on the earth. They ran on for two hours, till they had come to the thickest part of the forest; then some way before them Lubin began to see a light shining. It came from a small square house in a court-yard, and round the court-yard lay a deep moat; only one narrow plank led over and up to the entrance.

The red shoes, carrying the dead man, walked over, and Lubin followed them. When they were at the other side they turned, facing towards the plank that they had crossed, and Lubin seemed to read in the dead man's eye what he was to do.

Then he turned and lifted the plank away from over the moat, so that there was no longer any entrance or exit to the place. Through the window of the house he could see the three fiddlers quarrelling over the dead man's gold.

The red shoes went on, carrying their dead owner, till they got to the threshold, and there stopped. Then Lubin came and clicked up the latch, and pushed open the door, and in walked the dead man with the dagger sticking out of his heart.

The three fiddlers, when they saw that sight, dropped their gold and leapt out of the window; and as they fled, shrieking, thinking to cross the moat by the plank-bridge that was no longer there, one after the other they fell into the water, and, clutching each other by the throat, were drowned.

But the red shoes stayed where they were, and, tilting up his feet, let the traveller go gently upon the ground; and when Lubin held down the lantern to his face, on it lay a good smile, to tell him that the dead man thanked him for all he had done.

So in the morning Lubin went and fetched a priest to pray for the repose of the traveller's soul, and to give him good burial; and to him he gave all the dead man's money, but for himself he took the red shoes with the pointed toes, and set out to make his fortune in the world.

Walking along he found that however far he went he never grew tired. When he had gone on for more than a hundred miles, he came to the capital where the King lived with his Court.

All the flags of the city were at half-mast, and all the people were in half-mourning. Lubin asked at the first inn where he stopped what it all meant.

"You must indeed be a stranger," said his host, "not to know, for 'tis now nearly a year since this trouble began; and this very night more cause for mourning becomes due."

"Tell me of it, then," said Lubin, "for I know nothing at all."

"At least," returned the innkeeper, "you will know how, a little more than a year ago, the Queen, who was the most beautiful woman in the world, died, leaving the King with twelve daughters, who, after her, were reckoned the fairest women on earth, though the King says that all their beauty rolled into one would not equal that of his dead wife; and, indeed, poor man, there is no doubt that he loved her devotedly during her life, and mourns for her continually now she is dead."

"Only a small part of all this have I known," said Lubin.

"Well, but at least," said the innkeeper, "you will have heard how the Princesses were famed for their hair; so beautiful it was, so golden, and so long! And now, at every full moon, one of them goes bald in a night; and bald her head stays as a stone, for never an inch of hair grows on it again; and with her hair all her beauty goes pale, so that she is but the shadow of her former self—a thin-blooded thing, as if a vampire had come and sucked out half her life. Yes; ten months this has happened, and ten of the Princesses have lost their looks and their hair as well; and now only the Princess Royal and the youngest of all remain untouched; and doubtless one of them is to lose her crop tonight."

"But how does it happen?" cried Lubin. "Is no one put to keep watch, to guard them from the thing being done?"

"Ah! you talk, you talk!" said the innkeeper. "How? The King has offered half his kingdom to anyone who can tell him how the mischief is done; and the other half to the man who will put an end to it. To put it shortly, if you believe yourself a clever enough man, you may have the King for your father-in-law, with the pick of his daughters for your bride, and be his heir and lord of all when he dies!"

"For such a reward," said Lubin, "has no man made the attempt?"

"Aye, one a month; every time there has been some man fool enough to think himself so clever; and he has been turned out of the palace next day with his ears cropped."

"I will risk having my ears cropped," said Lubin; for his heart was sorry for the young Princesses, and the vanishing of their beauty. So he went up and knocked at the gates of the palace.

They went and told the King that a new man had come willing and wanting to have his ears cropped on the morrow. "Well, well," said the King, "let the poor fool in!" for indeed he had given up all hope. From the King Lubin heard the whole story over again. The old man sighed so it took him whole hours to tell it.

"I would be glad to be your son," said Lubin, when the King had ended; "but I would like better to make you rid of your sorrow."

"That is kind of you," said the King. "Perhaps I will only crop one of your ears tomorrow."

"When may one see the Princesses?" asked Lubin.

"They will be down to supper, presently," answered the King; "then you shall see them, what there is left of them."

Though it was reckoned that the next day Lubin would have to be drummed out of the palace with his ears cropped short, on this day he was to be treated like an honoured guest. When they went in to supper the King made him sit upon his right hand.

The twelve Princesses came in, their heads bowed down with weeping; all were fair, but ten of them were thin and pale, and wore white wimples over their heads like nuns; only the Princess Royal, who was the eldest, and Princess Lyneth, who was the youngest, had gold hair down to their feet, and were both so shiningly beautiful that the poor cobbler was altogether dazzled by the sight of them.

The King looked out of the window and said: "Heigho! There is the full moon beginning to rise." Then they all said grace and sat down.

But when the viands were handed round, all the Princesses sat weeping into their plates, and seemed unable to eat anything. For the pale and thin ones said: "Tonight another of our sisters will lose her golden hair and her good looks, and be like us!" Therefore they wept.

And Lyneth said: "Tonight, either my dear sister or myself will fall under the spell!" Therefore she wept more than the other ten. But the Princess Royal sat trembling, and crying:

"Tonight I know that the curse is to fall upon me, and me only!" Therefore she wept more than all.

Lubin sat, and watched, and listened, with his head bent down over his golden plate. "Which of these two shall I try most to save?" he thought. "How shall I test them, so as to know? If I could only tell which of them was to lose her hair tonight, then I might do something."

14

He saw that the youngest sister cried so much that she could eat nothing; but the Princess Royal, between her bursts of grief, picked up a morsel now and again from her plate, and ate it as though courage or despair reminded her that she must yet strive to live.

When the meat-courses were over, the King said to the Princesses: "I wish you would try to eat a little pudding! Here is a very promising youth, who is determined by all that is in him that harm shall happen to none of you tonight."

"Tomorrow he will be sent away with his ears cut short!" said Princess Lyneth; and her tears, as she spoke, ran down over the edge of her plate on to the cloth.

When supper was over the Princess Royal came up to Lubin, and said: "Do not be angry with my sister for what she said! It has only been too true of many who came before; tonight, unless you do better than them all, I shall lose my hair. It has been a wonder to me how I have been spared so long, seeing that I am the eldest, and, as some will have it, the fairest. Will you keep a good guard over me tonight, as though you knew for certain that I am to be the one this time to suffer?"

"I will guard you as my own life," said Lubin, "if you will but do as I ask you."

"Pledge yourself to me, then, in this cup!" said she, and lifted to his lips a bowl of red wine. Over the edge of it her eyes shone beautifully; he drank gazing into their clear depth.

"Where am I to be for the night," he asked of the King, "so that I may watch over the two Princesses?"

The King took him to a chamber with two further doors that opened out of it. "Here," said the King, "you are to sleep, and in the inner rooms sleep the Princess Royal and the Princess Lyneth. There is no entrance or exit to them but through this; therefore, when you are here with your door bolted, one would suppose that you had them safe. Alas! ten other men have tried like you to ward off the harm, and have failed; and so today I have ten daughters with no looks left to them, and no hair upon their heads."

As they were speaking, the two Princesses, with their sisters, came up to bed. And the pale ones, wearing their white wimples, came and kissed the golden hair of the other two, crying over it, and saying, "To one of you we are saying good-bye; tomorrow one of you will be like us!" Then they went away to their sleeping-place, and the Princess Royal and Lyneth kissed each other, and parted weeping, each into her own chamber.

"Watch well over us!" said Lyneth to Lubin, as she passed through. "Watch over me!" said the Princess Royal. And then the two doors were closed.

Lubin said to the King, "Could I now see the two Princesses, without being seen by them, it would help me to know what to do."

"Come down to my cabinet," said the King. "I have an invisible cap there, that I can lend you if you think you can do any good with it." So they went; and the King reached down the cap from the wall and gave it to Lubin.

"Now, good night, your Majesty," said Lubin; "I will do for you all I can."

The King answered, "Either you shall be my son-in-law tomorrow, or you shall have no ears. My wishes are with you that the former state may be yours."

Lubin went into his chamber and closed and bolted the door; then he put the bed up against it. "Now, at least," he thought, "there are three of us, and no more!" He put on his invisible cap, and going softly to the Princess Royal's door, opened it and peeped in.

She stood up before her glass, combing out her long gold hair, and smiling proudly because of its beauty. She gathered it up by all its ends and kissed it; then, letting it fall, she went on combing as before.

Lubin went out, closing the door again; then he took off his cap and knocked, and presently he heard the Princess Royal saying, "Come in!" She was lying down upon the bed, squeezing her eyes with her hands.

"Princess," he said, "I will watch over you like my own life, if you will do what I bid you. I am but a poor man, and the best that I can do is but poor; but I think, if you will, I can save your head from becoming as bare as a billiard ball."

The Princess asked him how.

"You know," said he, "that tonight something is to happen to one of you" ("To me!" said the Princess), "and all your hair will be stolen in such a way that nothing will ever make it grow again. See, here I have a pair of common scissors; let me but cut your hair close off all over your head, and then who can steal it? For a few months you will be a fright, but it can grow again."

"I think you are a silly fellow!" said the Princess. "Better for you to get to bed, and have your ears cropped quietly in the morning! After all, it may be my sister's turn to lose her hair, not mine. I shall not make myself a fright for a year of my life in order to save you."

"If you think so poorly of my offer," said Lubin, "I had better go to bed and sleep, and not trouble the Princess Lyneth at all with it."

"No, indeed!" said the Princess Royal. "Go to bed and sleep, poor fool!" And, in truth, Lubin was feeling so sleepy that he could hardly keep open his eyes.

Then he left her, and, pulling the invisible cap once more over his head, crept softly into Princess Lyneth's chamber.

17

She was standing before her glass with all her beautiful hair flowing down from shoulders to feet; and tears were falling fast out of her eyes as she kept drawing her hair together in her hands, kissing and moaning over it.

Then Lubin went out again, and, taking off his cap, knocked softly at the door.

"Come in!" said the Princess; and when he went in she was still standing before the glass weeping and moaning for her beautiful hair, that might never see another day. On the bed was lying a white wimple, ready for her to put on when her head was become bald.

"Princess," said Lubin, very humbly, "will you help me to save your beautiful hair, by doing what I ask?"

"What is it that you ask?" said she.

"Only this," he answered; "I am a poor man, and cannot do much for you, but only my best. Tonight you or your sister must lose your hair; and we know that afterwards, if that happen, it can never grow again. Now, come, here I have a common pair of scissors; if I could cut your hair quite short, in a few months it will grow again, and there will be nothing tonight that the Fates can steal. Will you let me do this for you in true service?"

The Princess looked at him, and looked at her glass. "Oh, my hair, my hair!" she moaned. Then she said, "What matters it? You mean to be good to me, and a month is the most that my fortune can last. If I do not lose it tonight, I lose it at the next full moon!" Then she shut her eyes and bade him take off all he wished. When he had finished, she picked up the wimple and covered her head with it; but Lubin took up the long coil of gold hair and wound it round his heart.

He knelt down at her feet. "Princess," he said, "be sure now that I can save you! Only I have one other request to make."

"What is that?" asked the Princess.

He took off one of his red shoes with the pointed toes. "Will you, for a strange thing, put on this shoe and wear it all tonight in your sleep? And in the morning I will ask you for it again."

The Princess promised faithfully that she would do so. Even before he had left the room she had put foot in it, promising that only he should take it off again.

Lubin's eyes were shut down with sleep as he groped his way to bed; he lay down with the other red shoe upon his foot. "Watch for your fellow!" he said to it; and then his senses left him and he was fast asleep.

In the middle of the night, while he was deep in slumber, the red shoe caught him by the foot and yanked him out of bed; he woke up to find himself standing in the middle of the room, and there before him stood the two doors of the inner chambers open; through that of the Princess Royal came a light. He heard the Princess Lyneth getting very softly out of her bed, and presently she stood in the doorway, with her hands out and her eyes fast shut; and the red shoe was on one foot, and the white wimple on her head. Little tears were running down from under her closed lids; and she sighed continually in her sleep. "Have pity on me!" she said.

She crossed slowly from one door to the other; and Lubin, putting on his invisible cap, crept softly after her. The Princess Royal's chamber was empty, but her glass was opened away from the wall like a door, and beyond lay a passage and steps. At the top of the steps was another door, and through it light came, and the sound of a soft voice singing.

Princess Lyneth, knowing nothing in her sleep, passed along the passage and up the steps till she came to the further doorway. Looking over her shoulder Lubin saw the Princess Royal sitting before a loom. In it lay a great cloth of gold like a bride's mantle, into which she was weaving the last threads of her skein. Close to her side lay a pair of great shears that shone like blue fire; and while she sang they opened and snapped, keeping time to the music she made.

Without ever turning her head the Princess Royal sat passing her fingers along the woof and crying:

> "Sister, sister, bring me your hair,
>   Of our Mother's beauty give me your share.
>   You must grow pale, while I must grow fair!"

And while she was so singing, Lyneth drew nearer and nearer, with her eyes fast shut, and the white wimple over her head. "Have pity on me!" she said, speaking in her sleep.

As soon as the Princess Royal heard that she laughed for joy, and catching up the great flaming shears, turned herself round to where Lyneth was standing. Then she opened the shears, and took hold of the wimple, and pulled it down.

All in a moment she was choking with rage, for horrible was the sight that met her eye. "Ah! cobbler's son," cried she, "you shall die for this! Tomorrow not only shall you have your two ears cropped, but you shall die: do not be afraid!"

Lubin looked at her and smiled, knowing how little she thought that he heard her words. "Ah! Princess Royal," he said to himself, "there is another who should now be afraid, but is not."

Then for very spite the Princess began slapping her sister's face. "Ah! wicked little sister," she cried, "you have cheated me this time! But go back and wait till your hair has grown,

and then my gown of gold shall be finished, although this once you have been too sly!" She threw down the shears, and drove her sister back by stair and passage, and through the looking-glass door at the other end.

Lubin following, stayed first to watch how by a secret spring the Princess Royal closed the mirror back into the wall; then he slipped on before, and taking his cap off, lay down on his bed pretending to be fast asleep. He heard Princess Lyneth return to her couch, and then came the Princess Royal and ground her teeth at him in the darkness.

Presently she, too, returned to her bed and lay down; and an hour after Lubin got up very softly and went into her chamber. There she lay asleep, with her beautiful hair all spread out upon the pillow; but Lubin had Princess Lyneth's hair wound round his heart. He touched the secret spring, so that the mirror opened to him, and he passed through toward the little chamber where stood the loom.

There hung the cloth of gold, all but finished; beside it the shears opened and snapped, giving out a blue light. He took up the shears in his hand, and pulled down the gold web from the loom, and back he went, closing the mirror behind him.

Then he came to the Princess Royal as she lay asleep; and first he laid the cloth of gold over her, and saw how at once she became ten times more fair than she was by rights, as fair almost as her dead mother, lacking one part only. But her beauty did not win him to have pity on her.

"There can be thieves, it seems, in high places!" he said; and with that he opened the shears over her head and let them snap: then all her long hair came out by the roots, and she lay white and withered before his eyes, and as bald as a stone.

He gathered up all her hair with one hand, and the cloth

of gold with the other, and went quietly away. Then, hiding the shears in a safe place, first he burnt the Princess Royal's hair, till it became only a little heap of frizzled cinders; and after that he went to the chamber of the ten Princesses, whose hair and whose sweet youth had been stolen from them. There they lay all in a row in ten beds, with pale, gentle faces, asleep under their white wimples.

He went to the first, and, laying the cloth of hair over her, cried:

"Sister, sister, I bring you your hair,
Of your Mother's beauty I give you your share.
One must grow pale, but you must grow fair!"

And as he said the words one part of the cloth unwove itself from the rest, and ran in ripples up the coverlet, and on to the pillow where the Princess's head lay. There it coiled itself under the wimple, a great mass of shining gold, and the face of the Princess flushed warm and lovely in her sleep.

Lubin passed on to the next bed, and there uttered the same words; and again one part of the web came loose, and wound itself about the sleeper's face, that grew warm and lovely at its touch. So he went from bed to bed, and when he came to the end there was no more of the web left.

He went back into his own chamber, laughing in his heart for joy, and there he dropped himself between the sheets and fell into a sound slumber.

He was awakened in the morning by the King knocking and trying to get into the room. Lubin pulled back the bed, and in came the King with a mournful countenance.

"Which of them is it?" said he.

"Go and ask them!" said Lubin.

22

The King went over and knocked at the Princess Royal's door: the knocking opened her eyes. Lubin heard her suddenly utter a yell. "Ah! now she has looked at herself in the glass," thought he.

"What is the matter?" called the King. "Come out and let me look at you!" But the Princess Royal would not come out. She ran quick to her mirror, and touched the secret spring. "At least," she thought, "though fiends have robbed me of all my beauty, I can get it back by wearing the cloth woven from my sisters' hair!" She skipped along the passage and up the steps to the little chamber where the loom was.

The King, getting no answer, went across and knocked at Lyneth's door; she came out, all fresh in her beauty, but wearing upon her head the wimple. "Ah!" said the King dolorously; and he snipped his fingers at Lubin.

Lubin laughed out. "But look at her face!" he said. "Surely she is beautiful enough?"

The Princess lifted up her wimple, and showed the King her hair all shorn beneath. "That was my doing," said Lubin; "'twas the way of saving it."

"What a Dutchman's remedy!" cried the King; and just then the Princess Royal's door flew open.

She came out tearing herself to pieces with rage; her face was pale and thin, and her head was as bare as a billiard ball. "Have that clown of a cobbler killed!" she cried in a passion. "That fool, that numbskull, that cheat! Have him beheaded, I say!"

"No, no, I am only to have one of my ears cropped off!" said Lubin, looking hard at her all the time.

"I am not at all sure," said the King. "You have done foolishly and badly, for not only have you let the disease go on, but your very remedy is as bad. Two heads of hair gone in one night! You had better have kept away. If the Princesses

23

wish it, certainly I will have you put to death."

"Will you not see the other Princesses too?" asked Lubin. "Let them decide between them whether I am to live or die!"

The King was just going to call for them, when suddenly the ten Princesses opened the door of their chamber, and stood before him shining like stars, with all their golden hair running down to their feet.

"Now put me to death!" said Lubin; and all the time he kept his eye upon the Princess Royal, who turned flame-coloured with rage.

"No, indeed!" cried the King. "Now you must be more than pardoned! You see, my dears," he said to Lyneth and the Princess Royal, "though you have suffered, your sisters have recovered all that they lost. They are ten to two; and I can't go back on arithmetic; I am bound to do even more than pardon him for this."

"Indeed and indeed yes!" replied the Princess Lyneth. "He has done ten times more than we thought of asking him!" And she went from one to another of her recovered sisters, kissing their beautiful long hair for pure gladness of heart. But when she came to the Princess Royal, she kissed her many times, and stooped down her face, upon her shoulder, and cried over her.

"Tell me now," said the King to Lubin, "for you are a very wonderful fellow, how did it all happen?"

Lubin looked at the Princess Royal; after all he could not betray a lady's secret. "I cannot tell you," he said; "if I did, there would be a death in the family."

"Well," said the King, "however you may have done it, I own that you have earned your reward. You have only to choose now which of my daughters is to make you my son-in-law. From this day you shall be known as my heir." He ranged all the Princesses in line, according to their ages.

"Now choose," said the King, "and choose well!"

Lubin went up to the Princess Royal. "I won't have you!" he said, looking very hard at her; and the Princess Royal dropped her eyes. Then he went on to the next. "Sweet lady," he said, "I dare not ask one with such beautiful hair as yours to marry me, who am a poor cobbler's son." But all the while he had the Princess Lyneth's hair bound round his heart.

He went on from one to another, and of each he kissed the hand saying that she was too fair to marry him.

He came to Lyneth and knelt down at her feet. "Lyneth," he said, "will you give the poor cobbler back his shoe?"

Lyneth, looking in his eyes, saw all that he meant. "And myself in it," she said, "for you love me dearly!" She put her arms round his neck, and whispered, "You marry me because I am a fright, and have no hair!"

But Lubin said, "I have your hair all wound round my heart, making it warm!"

So they were married, and lived together more happily than cobbler and princess ever lived in the world before. And the cobbler dropped mending shoes: only his wife's shoes he always mended. Very soon Lyneth's hair grew again, more shining and beautiful than before; but the Princess Royal remained pale, and thin, and was bald to the day of her death.

The Crown's Warranty

IVE hundred years ago or more, a king died, leaving two sons: one was the child of his first wife, and the other of his second, who surviving him became his widow. When the king was dying he took off the royal crown which he wore, and set it upon the head of the elder born, the son of his first wife, and said to him: "God is the lord of the air, and of the water, and of the dry land: this gift cometh to thee from God. Be merciful, over whatsoever thou holdest power, as God is!" And saying these words he laid his hands upon the heads of his two sons and died.

Now this crown was no ordinary crown, for it was made of the gold brought by the Wise Men of the East when they came to worship at Bethlehem. Every king that had worn it since then had reigned well and uprightly, and had been loved by all his people; but only to himself was it known what virtue lay in his crown; and every king at dying gave it to his son with the same words of blessing.

So, now, the king's eldest son wore the crown; and his step-mother knew that her own son could not wear it while he lived, therefore she looked on and said nothing. Now he was known to all the people of his country, because of his right to the throne, as the king's son; and his brother, the child of the second wife, was called the queen's son. But as yet they were both young, and cared little enough for crowns.

After the king's death the queen was made regent till the

king's son should be come to a full age; but already the little king wore the royal crown his father had left him, and the queen looked on and said nothing.

More than three years went by, and everybody said how good the queen was to the little king who was not her own son; and the king's son, for his part, was good to her and to his step-brother, loving them both; and all by himself he kept thinking, having his thoughts guarded and circled by his golden crown, "How shall I learn to be a wise king, and to be merciful when I have power, as God is?"

So to everything that came his way, to his playthings and his pets, to his ministers and his servants, he played the king as though already his word made life and death. People watching him said, "Everything that has touch with the king's son loves him." They told strange tales of him: only in fairy books could they be believed, because they were so beautiful; and all the time the queen, getting a good name for herself, looked on and said nothing.

One night the king's son was lying half-asleep upon his bed, with wise dreams coming and going under the circle of his gold crown, when a mouse ran out of the wainscot and came and jumped up upon the couch. The poor mouse had turned quite white with fear and horror, and was trembling in every limb as it cried its news into the king's ear. "O king's son," it said, "get up and run for your life! I was behind the wainscot in the queen's closet, and this is what I heard: if you stay here, when you wake up tomorrow you will be dead!"

The king's son got up, and all alone in the dark night stole out of the palace, seeking safety for his dear life. He sighed to himself, "There was a pain in my crown ever since I wore it. Alas, mother, I thought you were too kind a step-mother to do this!"

Outside it was still winter: there was no warmth in the world, and not a leaf upon the trees. He wandered away and away, wondering where he should hide.

The queen, when her villains came and told her the king's son was not to be found, went and looked in her magic crystal to find trace of him. As soon as it grew light, for in the darkness the crystal could show her nothing, she saw many miles away the king's son running to hide himself in the forest. So she sent out her villains to search until they should find him.

As they went the sun grew hot in the sky, and birds began singing. "It is spring!" cried the messengers. "How suddenly it has come!" They rode on till they came to the forest.

The king's son, stumbling along through the forest under the bare boughs, thought, "Even here where shall I hide? Nowhere is there a leaf to cover me." But when the sun grew warm he looked up; and there were all the trees breaking into bud and leaf, making a green heaven above his head. So when he was too weary to go farther, he climbed into the largest tree he could find; and the leaves covered him.

The queen's messengers searched through all the forest but could not find him; so they went back to her empty handed, not having either the king's crown or his heart to show. "Fools!" she cried, looking in her magic crystal, "he was in the big sycamore under which you stopped to give your horses provender!"

The sycamore said to the king's son, "The queen's eye is on you; get down and run for your life till you get to the hollow tarn-stones among the hills! But if you stay here, when you wake tomorrow you will be dead."

When the queen's messengers came once more to the forest they found it all wintry again, and without leaf; only the sycamore was in full green, clapping its hands for joy in

the keen and bitter air.

The messengers searched, and beat down the leaves, but the king's son was not there. They went back to the queen. She looked long in her magic crystal, but little could she see; for the king's son had hidden himself in a small cave beside the tarn-stones, and into the darkness the crystal could not pry.

Presently she saw a flight of birds crossing the blue, and every bird carried a few crumbs of bread in its beak. Then she ran and called to her villains, "Follow the birds, and they will take you to where the little wizard is; for they are carrying bread to feed him, and they are all heading for the tarn-stones up on the hills."

The birds said to the king's son, "Now you are rested; we have fed you, and you are not hungry. The queen's eye is on you. Up, and run for your life! If you stay here, when you wake up tomorrow you will be dead."

"Where shall I go?" said the king's son. "Go," answered the birds, "and hide in the rushes on the island of the pool of sweet waters!"

When the queen's messengers came to the tarn-stones, it was as though five thousand people had been feeding: they found crumbs enough to fill twelve baskets full, lying in the cave; but no king's son could they lay their hands on.

The king's son was lying hidden among the rushes on the island of the great pool of sweet waters; and thick and fast came silver-scaled fishes, feeding him.

It took the queen three days of hard gazing in her crystal, before she found how the fishes all swam to a point among the rushes of the island in the pool of sweet waters, and away again. Then she knew: and running to her messengers she cried: "He is among the rushes on the island in the pool of sweet waters; and all the fishes are feeding him!"

The fishes said to the king's son: "The queen's eye is on you; up, and swim to shore, and away for your life! For if they come and find you here, when you wake tomorrow you will certainly be dead."

"Where shall I go?" asked the king's son. "Wherever I go, she finds me." "Go to the old fox who gets his poultry from the palace, and ask him to hide you in his burrow!"

When the queen's messengers came to the pool they found the fishes playing at *alibis* all about in the water; but nothing of the king's son could they see.

The king's son came to the fox, and the fox hid him in his burrow, and brought him butter and eggs from the royal dairy. This was better fare than the king's son had had since the beginning of his wanderings, and he thanked the fox warmly for his friendship. "On the contrary," said the fox, "I am under an obligation to you; for ever since you came to be my guest I have felt like an honest man." "If I live to be king," said the king's son, "you shall always have butter and eggs from the royal dairy, and be as honest as you like."

The queen hugged her magic crystal for a whole week, but could make nothing out of it: for her crystal showed her nothing of the king's son's hiding-place, nor of the fox at his nightly thefts of butter and eggs from the royal dairy. But it so happened that this same fox was a sort of half-brother of the queen's; and so guilty did he feel with his brand-new good conscience that he quite left off going to see her. So in a little while the queen, with her suspicions and her magic crystal, had nosed out the young king's hiding-place.

The fox said to the king's son: "The queen's eye is on you! Get out and run for your life, for if you stay here till tomorrow, you will wake up and find yourself a dead goose!"

"But where else can I go to?" asked the king's son. "Is

there any place left for me?" The fox laughed, and winked, and whispered a word; and all at once the king's son got up and went.

The queen had said to her messengers, "Go and look in the fox's hole; and you shall find him!" But the messengers came and dug up the burrow, and found butter and eggs from the royal dairy, but of the king's son never a sign.

The king's son came to the palace, and as he crept through the gardens he found there his little brother alone at play,— playing sadly because now he was all alone. Then the king's son stopped and said, "Little brother, do you so much wish to be king?" And taking off the crown, he put it upon his brother's head. Then he went on through underground ways and corridors, till he came to the palace dungeons.

Now a dungeon is a hard thing to get out of, but it is easy enough to get into. He came to the deepest and darkest dungeon of all, and there he opened the door, and went in and hid himself.

The queen's son came running to his mother, wearing the king's crown. "Oh, mother," he said, "I am frightened! while I was playing, my brother came looking all dead and white, and put this crown on my head. Take it off for me, it hurts!"

When the queen saw the crown on her son's head, she was horribly afraid; for that it should have so come there was the most unlikely thing of all. She fetched her crystal ball, and looked in, asking where the king's son might be, and, for answer, the crystal became black as night.

Then said the queen to herself, "He is dead at last!"

But, now that the king's crown was on the wrong head, the air, and the water, and the dry land, over which God is lord, heard of it. And the trees said, "Until the king's son returns, we will not put forth bud or leaf!"

And the birds said, "We will not sing in the land, or breed or build nests until the king's son returns!"

And the fishes said, "We will not stay in the ponds or rivers to get caught, unless the king's son, to whom we belong, returns!"

And the foxes said, "Unless the king's son returns, we will increase and multiply exceedingly and be like locusts in the land!"

So all through that land the trees, though it was spring, stayed as if it were mid-winter; and all the fishes swam down to the sea; and all the birds flew over the sea, away into other countries; and all the foxes increased and multiplied, and became like locusts in the land.

Now when the trees, and the birds, and the beasts, and the fishes led the way the good folk of the country discovered that the queen was a criminal. So, after the way of the flesh, they took the queen and her little son, and bound them, and threw them into the deepest and darkest dungeon they could find; and said they: "Until you tell us where the king's son is, there you stay and starve!"

The king's son was playing all alone in his dungeon with the mice who brought him food from the palace larder, when the queen and her son were thrown down to him fast bound, as though he were as dangerous as a den of lions. At first he was terribly afraid when he found himself pursued into his last hiding-place; but presently he gathered from the queen's remarks that she was quite powerless to do him harm.

"Oh, what a wicked woman I am!" she moaned; and began crying lamentably, as if she hoped to melt the stone walls which formed her prison.

Presently her little son cried, "Mother, take off my brother's crown; it pricks me!" And the king's son sat in his corner, and

cried to himself with grief over the harm that his step-mother's wickedness had brought about.

"Mother," cried the queen's son again, "night and day since I have worn it, it pricks me; I cannot sleep!"

But the queen's heart was still hard; not if she could help, would she yet take off from her son the crown.

Hours went by, and the queen and her son grew hungry. "We shall be starved to death!" she cried. "Now I see what a wicked woman I am!"

"Mother," cried the queen's son, "someone is putting food into my mouth!" "No one," said the queen, "is putting any into mine. Now I know what a wicked woman I am!"

Presently the king's son came to the queen also, and began feeding her. "Someone is putting food into *my* mouth, now!" cried the queen. "If it is poisoned I shall die in agony! I wish," she said, "I wish I knew your brother were not dead; if I have killed him what a wicked woman I am!"

"Dear step-mother," said the king's son, "I am not dead, I am here."

"Here?" cried the queen, shaking with fright. "Here? not dead! How long have you been here?"

"Days, and days, and days," said the king's son, sadly.

"Ah! if I had only known *that*!" cried the queen. "*Now* I know what a wicked woman I am!"

Just then, the trap-door in the roof of the dungeon opened, and a voice called down, "Tell us where is the king's son! If you do not tell us, you shall stay here and starve."

"The king's son is here!" cried the queen.

"A likely story!" answered the gaolers. "Do you think we are going to believe that?" And they shut-to the trap.

The queen's son cried, "Dear brother, come and take back your crown, it pricks so!" But the king's son only undid the queen's bonds and his brother's. "Now," said he, "you are free: you can kill me now."

"Oh!" cried the queen, "what a wicked woman I must be! Do you think I could do it now?" Then she cried, "O little son, bring your poor head to me, and I will take off the crown!" and she took off the crown and gave it back to the king's son. "When I am dead," she said, "remember, and be kind to him!"

The king's son put the crown upon his own head.

Suddenly, outside the palace, all the land broke into leaf; there was a rushing sound in the river of fishes swimming up from the sea, and all the air was loud and dark with flights of returning birds. Almost at the same moment the foxes began to disappear and diminish, and cease to be like locusts in the land.

People came running to open the door of the deepest and darkest dungeon in the palace: "For either," they cried, "the queen is dead, or the king's son has been found!"

"Where is the king's son, then?" they called out, as they threw wide the door. "He is here!" cried the king; and out he came, to the astonishment of all, wearing his crown, and leading his step-mother and half-brother by the hand.

He looked at his step-mother, and she was quite white; as white as the mouse that had jumped upon the king's bed at midnight bidding him fly for his life. Not only her face, but her hair, her lips, and her very eyes were white and colourless, for she had gone blind from gazing too hard into her crystal ball, and hunting the king's son to death.

So she remained blind to the end of her days; but the king was more good to her than gold, and as for his brother, never did half-brothers love each other better than these. Therefore they all lived very happily together, and after a long time, the queen learned to forget what a wicked woman she had been.

Japonel

HERE was once upon a time a young girl named Japonel, the daughter of a wood-cutter, and of all things that lived by the woodside, she was the most fair.

Her hair in its net was like a snared sunbeam, and her face like a spring over which roses leaned down and birds hung fluttering to drink—such being the in-dwelling presence of her eyes and her laughing lips and her cheeks.

Whenever she crossed the threshold of her home, the birds and the flowers began calling to her, "Look up, Japonel! Look down, Japonel!" for the sight of the sweet face they loved so much. The squirrel called over its bough, "Look up, Japonel!" and the rabbit from between the roots, "Japonel, look down!" And Japonel, as she went, looked up and looked down, and laughed, thinking what a sweet-sounding place the world was.

Her mother, looking at her from day to day, became afraid: she said to the wood-cutter, "Our child is too fair; she will get no good of it."

But her husband answered, "Good wife, why should it trouble you? What is there in these quiet parts that can harm her? Keep her only from the pond in the wood, lest the pond-witch see her and become envious."

"Do not go near water, or you may fall in!" said her mother one day as she saw Japonel bending down to look at her face in a rain-puddle by the road.

Japonel laughed softly. "O silly little mother, how can I fall into a puddle that is not large enough for my two feet to stand in?"

But the mother thought to herself, when Japonel grows older and finds the pond in the wood, she will go there to look at her face, unless she has something better to see it in at home. So from the next pedlar who came that way she bought a little mirror and gave it to Japonel, that in it she might see her face with its spring-like beauty, and so have no cause to go near the pond in the wood. The lovely girl, who had never seen a mirror in her life, took the rounded glass in her hand and gazed for a long time without speaking, wondering more and more at her own loveliness. Then she went softly away with it into her own chamber, and wishing to find a name for a thing she loved so much, she called it, "Stream's eye", and hung it on the wall beside her bed.

In the days that followed, the door of her chamber would be often shut, and her face seldom seen save of herself alone. And "Look up, Japonel! Look down, Japonel!" was a sound she no longer cared to hear as she went through the woods; for the memory of "Stream's eye" was like a dream that clung to her, and floated in soft ripples on her face.

She grew tall like an aspen, and more fair, but pale. Her mother said, "Woe is me, for now I have made her vain through showing her her great beauty." And to Japonel herself she said, "Oh, my beautiful, my bright darling, though I have made thee vain, I pray thee to punish me not. Do not go near the pond in the wood to look in it, or an evil thing will happen to thee." And Japonel smiled dreamily amid half-thoughts, and kissing her mother, "Dear mother," she said, "does 'Stream's eye' tell me everything of my beauty, or am I in other eyes still fairer?" Then her mother answered sadly,

"Nay, but I trust the open Eye of God finds in thee a better beauty than thy mirror can tell thee of."

Japonel, when she heard that answer, went away till she came to the pond in the wood. It lay down in a deep hollow, and drank light out of a clear sky, which, through a circle of dark boughs, ever looked down on it. "Perhaps," she said to herself, "it is here that God will open His Eye and show me how much fairer I am than even 'Stream's eye' can tell me." But she thought once of her mother's words, and went by.

Then she turned again, "It is only that my mother fears lest I become vain. What harm can come if I do look once? it will be in my way home." So she crept nearer and nearer to the pond, saying to herself, "To see myself once as fair as God sees me cannot be wrong. Surely that will not make me more vain." And when she came through the last trees, and stood near the brink, she saw before her a little old woman, dressed in green, kneeling by the water and looking in.

"There at least," she said to herself, "is one who looks in without any harm happening to her. I wonder what it is she sees that she stays there so still." And coming a little nearer, "Good dame," called Japonel, "what is it you have found there, that you gaze at so hard?" And the old woman, without moving or looking up, answered, "My own face; but a hundred times younger and fairer, as it was in my youth."

Then thought Japonel, "How should I look now, who am fair and in the full bloom of my youth? It is because my mother fears lest I shall become vain that she warned me." So she came quickly and knelt down by the old woman and looked in. And even as she caught sight of her face gazing up, pale and tremulous ("Quick, go away!" its lips seemed to be saying), the old woman slid down from the bank and caught hold of her reflection with green, weed-like arms, and drew it away into the pool's still depths below. Beneath

Japonel's face lay nothing now but blank dark water, and far away in, a faint face gazed back beseeching, and its lips moved with an imprisoned prayer that might not make itself heard. Only three bubbles rose to the surface, and broke into three separate sighs like the shadow of her own name. Then the pond-witch stirred the mud, and all trace of that lost image went out, and Japonel was left alone.

She rose, expecting to see nothing, to be blind; but the woods were there, night shadows were gathering to their tryst under the boughs, and brighter stars had begun blotting the semi-brightness of the sky. All the way home she went feebly, not yet resolved of the evil that had come upon her. She stole quietly to her own little room in the fading light, and took down "Stream's eye" from the wall. Then she fell forward upon the bed, for all the surface of her glass was grown blank: never could she hope to look upon her own face again.

The next morning she hung her head low, for she feared all her beauty was flown from her, till she heard her father say, "Wife, each day it seems to me our Japonel grows more fair." And her mother answered, sighing, "She is too fair, I know."

Then Japonel set out once more for the pond in the wood. As she went the birds and the flowers sang to her, "Look up, Japonel; look down, Japonel!" but Japonel went on, giving them no heed. She came to the water's side, and leaning over, saw far down in a tangle of green weeds a face that looked back to hers, faint and blurred by the shimmering movement of the water. Then, weeping, she wrung her hands and cried:

> "Ah! sweet face of Japonel,
> Beauty and grace of Japonel,
> Image and eyes of Japonel,
> 'Come back!' sighs Japonel."

And bubble by bubble a faint answer was returned that broke like a sob on the water's surface:

> "I am the face of Japonel,
>   The beauty and grace of Japonel;
>   Here under a spell, Japonel,
>   I dwell, Japonel."

All day Japonel cried so, and was so answered. Now and again, green weeds would come skimming to the surface, and seem to listen to her reproach, and then once more sink down to their bed in the pond's depths, and lie almost still, waving long slimy fingers through the mud.

The next day Japonel came again, and cried as before:

> "Ah! sweet face of Japonel.
>   Beauty and grace of Japonel,
>   Image and eyes of Japonel,
>   'Come back!' cries Japonel."

And her shadow in the water made answer:

> "I am the face of Japonel,
>   The beauty and grace of Japonel;
>   Here under a spell, Japonel,
>   I dwell, Japonel."

Now as she sat and sorrowed she noticed that whenever a bird flew over the pond it dropped something out of its mouth into the water, and looking she saw millet-seeds lying everywhere among the weeds of its surface; one by one they were being sucked under by the pond-witch.

Japonel stayed so long by the side of the pond, that on her

way home it had fallen quite dark while she was still in the middle of the wood. Then all at once she heard a bird with loud voice cry out of the darkness, "Look up, Japonel!" The cry was so sudden and so strange, coming at that place and that hour, that all through her grief she heard it, and stopped to look up. Again in the darkness she heard the bird cry, "Why do you weep, Japonel?" Japonel said, "Because the pond-witch has carried away my beautiful reflection in the water, so that I can see my own face no more."

Then the bird said, "Why have you not done as the birds do? She is greedy; so they throw in millet-seeds, and then she does not steal the reflection of their wings when they pass over." And Japonel answered, "Because I did not know that, therefore I am today the most miserable of things living." Then said the bird, "Come tomorrow, and you shall be the happiest."

So the next day Japonel went and sat by the pond in the wood, waiting to be made the happiest, as the bird had promised her. All day long great flocks of birds went to and fro, and the pond became covered with seeds. Japonel looked; "Why, they are poppy-seeds!" she cried. (Now poppy-seeds when they are eaten make people sleep.) Just as the sun was setting all the birds began suddenly to cry in chorus, "Look down, Japonel! Japonel, look down!" And there, on the pond's surface, lay an old woman dressed in green, fast asleep, with all the folds of her dress and the wrinkles of her face full of poppy-seeds.

Then Japonel ran fast to the pond's edge and looked down. Slowly from the depth rose the pale beautiful reflection of herself, untying itself from the thin green weeds, and drifting towards the bank. It looked up with tremulous greeting, half sadness, half pleasure, seeming so glad after that long separation to return to its sweet mistress. So as it came and settled below her own face in the water, Japonel stooped down over it and kissed it.

Then she sprang back from the brink and ran home, fast, fast in the fading light. And there, when she looked in her mirror, was once more the beautiful face she loved, a little blue and wan from its long imprisonment under water. And so it ever remained, beautiful, but wan, to remind her of the sorrow that had come upon her when, loving this too well, she had not loved enough to listen to the cry of the birds: "Look up, Japonel!" and, "Japonel, look down!"

The Rooted Lover

ORNING and evening a ploughboy went driving his team through a lane at the back of the palace garden. Over the hedge the wind came sweet with the scents of a thousand flowers, and through the hedge shot glimpses of all the colours of the rainbow, while now and then went the sheen of silver and gold tissue when the Princess herself paced by with her maidens. Also above all the crying and calling of the blackbirds and thrushes that filled the gardens with song, came now and then an airy exquisite voice flooding from bower to field; and that was the voice of the Princess Fleur-de-lis herself singing.

When she sang all the birds grew silent; new flowers came into bud to hear her and into blossom to look at her; apples and pears ripened and dropped down at her feet; her voice sang the bees home as if it were evening: and the ploughboy as he passed stuck his face into the thorny hedge, and feasted his eyes and ears with the sight and sound of her beauty.

He was a red-faced boy, red with the wind and the sun: over his face his hair rose like a fair flame, but his eyes were black and bold, and for love he had the heart of a true gentleman.

Yet he was but a ploughboy, rough-shod and poorly clad in a coat of frieze, and great horses went at a word from him. But no word from him might move the heart of that great Princess; she never noticed the sound of his team as it jingled

42

by, nor saw the dark eyes and the bronzed red face wedged into the thorn hedge for love of her.

"Ah! Princess," sighed the ploughboy to himself, as the thorns pricked into his flesh, "were it but a thorn-hedge which had to be trampled down, you should be my bride tomorrow!" But shut off by the thorns, he was not a whit further from winning her than if he had been kneeling at her feet.

He had no wealth in all the world, only a poor hut with poppies growing at the door; no mother or father, and his own living to get. To think at all of the Princess was the sign either of a knave or a fool.

No knave, but perhaps a fool, he thought himself to be. "I will go," he said at last, "to the wise woman who tells fortunes and works strange cures, and ask her to help me."

So he took all the money he had in the world and went to the wise woman in her house by the dark pool, and said, "Show me how I may win Princess Fleur-de-lis to be my wife, and I will give you everything I possess."

"That is a hard thing you ask," said the wise woman; "how much dare you risk for it?"

"Anything you can name," said he.

"Your life?" said she.

"With all my heart," he replied; "for without her I shall but end by dying."

"Then," said the wise woman, "give me your money, and you shall take your own risk."

Then he gave her all.

"Now," said she, "you have but to choose any flower you like, and I will turn you into it; then, in the night I will take you and plant you in the palace garden; and if before you die the Princess touches you with her lips and lays you as a flower in her bosom, you shall become a man again and win her love; but if not, when the flower dies you will die too and be no more. So if that seem to you a good bargain, you have but to name your flower, and the thing is done."

"Agreed, with all my heart!" cried the ploughboy. "Only make me into some flower that is like me, for I would have the Princess to know what sort of a man I am, so that she shall not be deceived when she takes me to her bosom."

He looked himself up and he looked himself down in the pool which was before the wise woman's home; at his rough frieze coat with its frayed edges, his long supple limbs, and his red face with its black eyes, and hair gleaming at the top.

"I am altogether like a poppy," he said, "what with my red head, and my rough coat, and my life among fields which the plough turns to furrow. Make a poppy of me, and put me in the palace garden and I will be content."

Then she stroked him down with her wand full couthly, and muttered her wise saws over him, for she was a wonderful witch-woman; and he turned before her very eyes into a great red poppy, and his coat of frieze became green and hairy all over him, and his feet ran down into the ground like roots.

The wise woman got a big flower-pot and a spade; and she dug him up out of the ground and planted him in the pot, and having watered him well, waited till it was quite dark.

As soon as the pole-star had hung out its light she got across her besom, tucked the flower-pot under her arm, and sailed away over hedge and ditch till she came to the palace garden.

There she dug a hole in a border by one of the walks, shook the ploughboy out of his flower-pot, and planted him with his feet deep down in the soil. Then giving a wink all round, and a wink up to the stars, she set her cap to the east, mounted her besom, and rode away into thin space.

But the poppy stood up where she had left him taking care of his petals, so as to be ready to show them off to the Princess the next morning. He did not go fast asleep, but just dozed the time away, and found it quite pleasant to be a flower, the night being warm. Now and then small insects ran up his stalks, or a mole passed under his roots, reminding him of the mice at home. But the poppy's chief thought was for the morning to return; for then would come the Princess walking straight to where he stood, and would reach out a hand and gather him, and lay her lips to his and his head upon her bosom, so that in the shaking of a breath he could turn again to his right shape, and her love would be won for ever.

Morning came, and gardeners with their brooms and barrows went all about, sweeping up the leaves, and polishing off the slugs from the gravel-paths. The head gardener came and looked at the poppy. "Who has been putting this weed here?" he cried. And at that the poppy felt a shiver of red ruin go through him; for what if the gardener were to weed him up so that he could never see the Princess again?

All the other gardeners came and considered him, twisting wry faces at him. But they said, "Perhaps it is a whim of the Princess's. It's none of our planting." So after all they let him be.

The sun rose higher and higher, and the gardeners went carrying away their barrows and brooms; but the poppy stood waiting with his black eye turned to the way by which the Princess should come.

It was a long waiting, for princesses do not rise with the lark, and the poppy began to think his petals would be all shrivelled and old before she came. But at last he saw slim white feet under the green boughs and heard voices and shawm-like laughter and knew that it was the Princess coming to him.

Down the long walks he watched her go, pausing here and there to taste a fruit that fell or to look at a flower that opened. To him she would come shortly, and so bravely would he woo her with his red face, that she would at once bend down and press her lips to his, and lift him softly to her bosom. Yes, surely she would do this.

She came; she stopped full and began looking at him: he burned under her gaze. "That is very beautiful!" she said at last. "Why have I not seen that flower before? Is it so rare, then, that there is no other?" But, "Oh, it is too common!" cried all her maids in a chorus; "it is only a common poppy such as grows wild in the fields."

"Yet it is very beautiful," said the Princess; and she looked at it long before she passed on. She half bent to it. "Surely now," said the poppy, "her lips to mine!"

"Has it a sweet smell?" she asked. But one of her maids said, "No, only a poor little stuffy smell, not nice at all!" and the Princess drew back.

"Alas, alas," murmured the poor poppy in his heart, as he watched her departing, "why did I forget to choose a flower with a sweet smell? Then surely at this moment she would have been mine." He felt as if his one chance were gone, and death already overtaking him. But he remained brave; "At least," he said, "I will die looking at her; I will not faint or wither, till I have no life left in me. And after all there is tomorrow." So he went to sleep hoping much, and slept late into the morning of the next day.

Opening his eyes he was aware of a great blaze of red in a border to his right. Ears had been attentive to the words of Princess Fleur-de-lis, and a whole bed of poppies had been planted to gratify her latest fancy. There they were, in a thick mass burning the air around them with their beauty. Alas! against their hundreds what chance had he?

And the Princess came and stood by them, lost in admiration, while the poppy turned to her his love-sick eye, trying to look braver than them all. And she being gracious, and not forgetful of what first had given her pleasure, came and looked at him also, but not very long; and as for her lips, there was no chance for him there now. Yet for the delight of those few moments he was almost contented with the fate he had chosen—to be a flower, and to die as a flower so soon as his petals fell.

Days came and went; they were all alike now, save that the Princess stayed less often to look at him or the other poppies which had stolen his last chance from him. He saw autumn changes coming over the garden; flowers sickened and fell, and were removed, and the nights began to get cold.

Beside him the other poppies were losing their leaves, and their flaming tops had grown scantier; but for a little while he would hold out still; so long as he had life his eye should stay open to look at the Princess as she passed by.

The sweet-smelling flowers were gone, but the loss of their fragrant rivalry gave him no greater hopes: one by one every gorgeous colour dropped away; only when a late evening primrose hung her lamp beside him in the dusk did he feel that there was anything left as bright as himself to the eye. And now death was taking hold of him, each night twisting and shrivelling his leaves; but still he held up his head, determined that, though but for one more day, his eye should be blessed by a sight of his Princess. If he could keep looking at her he believed he should dream of her when dead.

At length he could see that he was the very last of all the poppies, the only spot of flame in a garden that had gone grey. In the cold dewy mornings cobwebs hung their silvery hammocks about the leaves, and the sun came through mist, making them sparkle. And beautiful they were, but to him they looked like the winding-sheet of his dead hopes.

Now it happened just about this time that the Prince of a neighbouring country was coming to the Court to ask Princess Fleur-de-lis' hand in marriage. The fame of his manners and his good looks had gone before him, and the Princess being bred to the understanding that princesses must marry for the good of nations according to the bidding of their parents, was willing, since the King her father wished it, to look upon his suit with favour. All that she looked for was to be wooed with sufficient ardour, and to be allowed time for a becoming hesitancy before yielding.

A great ball was prepared to welcome the Prince on his arrival; and when the day came, Princess Fleur-de-lis went into the garden to find some flower that she might wear as an adornment of her loveliness. But almost everything had died of frost, and the only flower that retained its full beauty was the poor bewitched poppy, kept alive for love of her.

"How wonderfully that red flower has lasted!" she said to one of her maidens. "Gather it for me, and I will wear it with my dress tonight."

The poppy, not knowing that he was about to meet a much more dangerous rival than any flower, thrilled and almost fainted for bliss as the maid picked him from the stalk and carried him in.

He lay upon Princess Fleur-de-lis' toilet-table and watched the putting on of her ballroom array. "If she puts me in her breast," he thought, "she must some time touch me with her lips; and then!"

And then, when the maid was giving soft finishing touches to the Princess's hair, the beloved one herself took up the poppy and arranged it in the meshes of gold. "Alas!" thought

48

the poppy, even while he nestled blissfully in its warm depths, "I shall never reach her lips from here; but I shall dream of her when dead; and for a ploughboy, that surely is enough of happiness."

So he went down with her to the ball, and could feel the soft throbbing of her temples, for she had not yet seen this Prince who was to be her lover, and her head was full of gentle agitation and excitement to know what he would be like. Very soon he was presented to her in state. Certainly he was extremely passable: he was tall and fine and had a pair of splendid mustachios that stuck out under his nostrils like walrus-tusks, and curled themselves like ram's horns. Beyond a slight fear that these might sweep her away when he tried to kiss her, she favoured his looks sufficiently to be prepared to accept his hand when he offered it.

Then music called to them invitingly, and she was led away to the dance.

As they danced the Prince said: "I cannot tell how it is, I feel as if someone were looking at me."

"Half the world is looking at you," said the Princess in slight mockery. "Do you not know you are dancing with Princess Fleur-de-lis?"

"Beautiful Princess," said the Prince, "can I ever forget it? But it is not in that way I feel myself looked at. I could swear I have seen somewhere a man with a sunburnt face and a bold black eye looking at me."

"There is no such here," said the Princess; and they danced on.

When the dance was over the Prince led her to a seat screened from view by rich hangings of silken tapestry; and Princess Fleur-de-lis knew that the time for the wooing was come.

She looked at him; quite clearly she meant to say "Yes."

Without being glad, she was not sorry. If he wooed well she would have him.

"It is strange," said the Prince, "I certainly feel that I am being looked at."

The Princess was offended. "I am not looking at you in the least," she said slightingly.

"Ah!" replied the other, "if you did, I should lose at once any less pleasant sensation; for when your eyes are upon me I know only that I love you—you, Princess, who are the most beautiful, the most radiant, the most accomplished, the most charming of your sex! Why should I waste time in laying my heart bare before you? It is here; it is yours. Take it!"

"Truly," thought the Princess, "this is very pretty wooing, and by no means ill done." She bent down her head, and she toyed and she coyed, but she would not say "Yes" yet.

But the poppy, when he heard the Prince's words, first went all of a tremble, and then giving a great jump fell down at the Princess's feet. And she, toying and coying, and not wishing to say "Yes" yet, bent down and taking up the poppy from where it had fallen, brushed it gently to and fro over her lips to conceal her smiles, and then tucking her chin down into the dimples of her neck began to arrange the flower in the bosom of her gown.

As she did so, all of a sudden a startled look came over her face. "Oh! I am afraid!" she cried. "The man, the man with the red face, and the strong black eyes!"

"What is the matter?" demanded the Prince, bending over her in the greatest concern.

"No, no!" she cried, "go away! Don't touch me! I can't and I won't marry you! Oh, dear! oh, dear! what is going to become of me?" And she jumped up and ran right away out of the ballroom, and up the great staircase, where she let the poppy fall, and right into her own room, where she barred and bolted herself in.

In the palace there was the greatest confusion: everybody was running about and shaking heads at everybody else. "Heads and tails! has it come to this?" cried the King, as he saw a party of serving-men turning out a ploughboy who by some unheard of means had found his way into the palace. Then he went up to interview his daughter as to her strange and sudden refusal of the Prince.

The Princess wrung her hands and cried: she didn't know why, but she couldn't help herself: nothing on earth should induce her to marry him.

Then the King was full of wrath, and declared that if she were not ready to obey him in three days' time, she should be turned out into the world like a beggar to find a living for herself.

So for three days the Princess was locked up and kept on nothing but bread and water; and every day she cried less, and was more determined than ever not to marry the Prince.

"Whom do you suppose you are going to marry then?" demanded the King in a fury.

"I don't know," said the Princess, "I only know he is a dear; and has got a beautiful tanned face and bold black eyes."

The King felt inclined to have all the tanned faces and bold black eyes in his kingdom put to death: but as the Princess's obstinacy showed no signs of abating, he ended by venting all his anger upon her. So on the third day she was clothed in rags, and had all her jewellery taken off her, and was turned out of the palace to find her way through the world alone.

And as she went on and on, crying and wondering what would become of her, she suddenly saw by the side of the road a charming cottage with winter poppies growing at the door. And in the doorway stood a beautiful man, with a tanned face and bold black eyes, looking as like a poppy as it was possible for a man to look.

Then he opened his arms: and the Princess opened her arms: and he ran, and she ran. And they ran and they ran and they ran, till they were locked in each other's arms, and lived happily ever after.

The Way of the Wind

HERE the world breaks up into islands among the blue waves of an eastern sea, in a little house by the seashore, lived Katipah, the only child of poor parents. When they died she was left quite alone and could not find a heart in the world to care for her. She was so poor that no man thought of marrying her, and so delicate and small that as a drudge she was worth nothing to anybody.

Once a month she would go and stand at the temple gate, and say to the people as they went in to pray, "Will nobody love me?" And the people would turn their heads away quickly and make haste to get past, and in their hearts would wonder to themselves: "Foolish little Katipah! Does she think that we can spare time to love anyone so poor and unprofitable as she?"

On the other days Katipah would go down to the beach, where everybody went who had a kite to fly—for all the men in that country flew kites, and all the children,—and there she would fly a kite of her own up into the blue air; and watching the wind carrying it farther and farther away, would grow quite happy thinking how a day might come at last when she would really be loved, though her queer little outside made her seem so poor and unprofitable.

Katipah's kite was green, with blue eyes in its square face; and in one corner it had a very small pursed-up red mouth holding a spray of peach-blossom. She had made it herself;

and to her it meant the green world, with the blue sky over it when the spring begins to be sweet; and there, tucked away in one corner of it, her own little warm mouth waiting and wishing to be kissed: and out of all that wishing and waiting the blossom of hope was springing, never to be let go.

All round her were hundreds of others flying their kites, and all had some wish or prayer to Fortune. But Katipah's wish and prayer were only that she might be loved.

The silver sandhills lay in loops and chains round the curve of the blue bay, and all along them flocks of gaily coloured kites hovered and fluttered and sprang. And, as they went up into the clear air, the wind sighing in the strings was like the crying of a young child. "Wahoo! wahoo!" every kite seemed to cradle the wailings of an invisible infant as it went mounting aloft, spreading its thin apron to the wind.

"Wahoo! wahoo!" sang Katipah's blue-and-green kite, "shall I ever be loved by anybody?" And Katipah, keeping fast hold of the string, would watch where it mounted and looked so small, and think that surely some day her kite would bring her the only thing she much cared about.

Katipah's next-door neighbour had everything that her own lonely heart most wished for: not only had she a husband, but a fine baby as well. Yet she was such a jealous, cross-grained body that she seemed to get no happiness out of the fortune Heaven had sent her. Husband and child seemed both to have caught the infection of her bitter temper; all day and night beating and brawling went on; there seemed no peace in that house.

But for all that the woman, whose name was Bimsha, was quite proud of being a wife and a mother: and in the daytime, when her man was away, she would look over the fence and laugh at Katipah, crying boastfully, "Don't think you will

54

ever have a husband, Katipah: you are too poor and unprofitable! Look at me, and be envious!"

Then Katipah would go softly away, and send up her kite by the seashore till she heard a far-off, sweet, babe-like cry as the wind blew through the strings high in air.

"Shall I ever be loved by anybody?" thought she, as she jerked at the cord; and away the kite flew higher than ever, and the sound of its call grew fainter.

One morning, in the beginning of the year, Katipah went up on to the hill under plum-boughs white with bloom, meaning to gather field-sorrel for her midday meal; and as she stooped with all her hair blowing over her face, and her skirts knotting and billowing round her pretty brown ankles, she felt as if someone had kissed her from behind.

"That cannot be," thought Katipah, with her fingers fast upon a stalk of field-sorrel; "it is too soon for anything so good to happen." So she picked the sorrel quietly, and put it into her basket. But now, not to be mistaken, arms came round her, and she *was* kissed.

She stood up and put her hands into her breast, quite afraid lest her little heart, which had grown so light, should be caught by a puff of wind and blown right away out of her bosom, and over the hill and into the sea, and be drowned.

And now her eyes would not let her doubt; there by her side stood a handsome youth, with quick-fluttering, posy-embroidered raiment. His long dark hair was full of white plum-blossoms, as though he had just pushed his head through the branches above. His hands also were loaded with the same, and they kept sifting out of his long sleeves whenever he moved his arms. Under the hem of his robe Katipah could see that he had heron's wings bound about his ankles.

"He must be very good," thought Katipah, "to be so

beautiful! and indeed he must be very good to kiss poor me!"

"Katipah," said the wonderful youth, "though you do not know me, I know you. It is I who so often helped you to fly your green kite by the shore. I have been up there, and have looked into its blue eyes, and kissed its little red mouth which held the peach-blossom. It was I who made songs in its strings for your heart to hear. I am the West Wind, Katipah—the wind that brings fine weather. 'Gamma-gata' you must call me, for it is I who bring back the wings that fly till the winter is over. And now I have come down to earth, to fetch you away and make you my wife. Will you come, Katipah?"

"I will come, Gamma-gata!" said Katipah, and she crouched and kissed the heron-wings that bound his feet; then she stood up and let herself go into his arms.

"Have you enough courage?" asked the West Wind.

"I do not know," answered Katipah, "for I have never tried."

"To come with me," said the Wind, "you need to have much courage; if you have not, you must wait till you learn it. But none the less for that shall you be the wife of Gamma-gata, for I am the gate of the wild geese, as my name says, and my heart is foolish with love of you," Gamma-gata took her up in his arms, and swung with her this way and that, tossing his way through blossom and leaf; and the sunlight became an eddy of gold round her, and wind and laughter seemed to become part of her being, so that she was all giddy and dazed and glad when at last Gamma-gata set her down.

"Stand still, my little one!" he cried—"stand still while I put on your bridal veil for you; then your blushes shall look like a rose-bush in snow!" So Katipah stood with her feet in the green sorrel, and Gamma-gata went up into the plum-tree and shook, till from head to foot she was showered with white blossom.

"How beautiful you seem to me!" cried Gamma-gata when he returned to ground.

Then he lifted her once more and set her in the top of a plum-tree, and going below, cried up to her, "Leap, little Wind-wife, and let me see that you have courage!"

Katipah looked long over the deep space that lay between them, and trembled. Then she fixed her eyes fast upon those of her lover, and leapt, for in the laughter of his eyes she had lost all her fear.

He caught her half-way in air as she fell. "You are not really brave," said he; "if I had shut my eyes you would not have jumped."

"If you had shut your eyes just then," cried Katipah, "I would have died for fear."

He set her once more in the tree-top, and disappeared from her sight. "Come down to me, Katipah!" she heard his voice calling all round her.

Clinging fast to the topmost bough, "Oh, Gamma-gata," she cried, "let me see your eyes, and I will come."

Then with darkened brow he appeared to her again out of his blasts, and took her in his arms and lifted her down a little sadly till her feet touched safe earth. And he blew away the beautiful veil of blossoms with which he had showered her, while Katipah stood like a shamed child and watched it go, shredding itself to pieces in the spring sunshine.

And Gamma-gata, kissing her tenderly, said: "Go home, Katipah, and learn to have courage! and when you have learned it I will be faithful and will return to you again. Only remember, however long we may be parted, and whatever winds blow ill-fortune up to your door, Gamma-gata will watch over you. For in deed and truth you are the wife of the West Wind now, and truly he loves you, Katipah!"

"Oh, Gamma-gata!" cried Katipah, "tell the other winds, when they come, to blow courage into me, and to blow me back to you: and do not let that be long!"

"I will tell them," said Gamma-gata; and suddenly he was gone. Katipah saw a drift of white petals borne over the tree-tops and away to sea, and she knew that there went Gamma-gata, the beautiful windy youth who, loving her so well, had made her his wife between the showers of the plum-blossom and the sunshine, and had promised to return to her as soon as she was fit to receive him.

So Katipah gathered up her field-sorrel, and went away home and ate her solitary midday meal with a mixture of pride and sorrow in her timid little breast. "Some day, when I am grown brave," she thought, "Gamma-gata will come back to me; but he will not come yet."

In the evening Bimsha looked over the fence and jeered at her. "Do not think, Katipah," she cried, "that you will ever get a husband, for all your soft looks! You are too poor and unprofitable."

Katipah folded her meek little body together like a concertina when it shuts, and squatted to earth in great contentment of spirit. "Silly Bimsha," said she, "I already have a husband, a fine one! Ever so much finer than yours!"

Bimsha turned pale and cold with envy to hear her say that, for she feared that Katipah was too good and simple to tell her an untruth, even in mockery. But she put a brave face upon the matter, saying only, "I will believe in that fine husband of yours when I see him!"

"Oh, you will see him," answered Katipah, "if you look high enough! But he is far away over *your* head, Bimsha; and you will not hear him beating me at night, for that is not his way!"

At this soft answer Bimsha went back into her house in a

fury, and Katipah laughed to herself. Then she sighed, and said, "Oh, Gamma-gata, return to me quickly, lest my word shall seem false to Bimsha, who hates me!"

Every day after this Bimsha thrust her face over the fence to say: "Katipah, where is this fine husband of yours? He does not seem to come home often."

Katipah answered slyly: "He comes home late, when it is dark, and he goes away very early, almost before it is light. It is not necessary for his happiness that he should see *you*."

"Certainly there is a change in Katipah," thought Bimsha: "she has become saucy with her tongue." But her envious heart would not allow her to let matters be. Night and morning she cried to Katipah, "Katipah, where is your fine husband?" And Katipah laughed at her, thinking to herself: "To begin with, I will not be afraid of anything Bimsha may say. Let Gamma-gata know that!"

And now every day she looked up into the sky to see what wind was blowing; but east, or north, or south, it was never the one wind that she looked for.

The east wind came from the sea, bringing rain, and beat upon Katipah's door at night. Then Katipah would rise and open it, and standing in the downpour, would cry, "East wind, east wind, go and tell your brother Gamma-gata that I am not afraid of you any more than I am of Bimsha!"

One night the east wind, when she said that, pulled a tile off Bimsha's house, and threw it at her; and Katipah ran in and hid behind the door in a great hurry. After that she had less to say when the east wind came and blew under her gable and rattled at her door. "Oh, Gamma-gata," she sighed, "if I might only set eyes on you, I would fear nothing at all!"

When the weather grew fine again Katipah returned to the shore and flew her kite as she had always done before the love of Gamma-gata had entered her heart. Now and then, as she did so, the wind would change softly, and begin blowing from the west. Then little Katipah would pull lovingly at the string, and cry, "Oh, Gamma-gata, have you got fast hold of it up there?"

One day after dusk, when she, the last of all the flyers, hauled down her kite to earth, there she found a heron's feather fastened among the strings. Katipah knew who had sent that, and kissed it a thousand times over; nor did she mind for many days afterwards what Bimsha might say, because the heron's feather lay so close to her heart, warming it with the hope of Gamma-gata's return.

But as weeks and months passed on, and Bimsha still did not fail to say each morning, "Katipah, where is your fine husband today?" The timid heart grew faint with waiting. "Alas!" thought Katipah, "if Heaven would only send me a child, I would show it to her; she would believe me easily then! However tiny, it would be big enough to convince her. Gamma-gata, it is a very little thing that I ask!"

And now every day and all day long she sent up her kite from the seashore, praying that a child might be born to her and convince Bimsha of the truth. Everyone said: "Katipah is mad about kite-flying! See how early she goes and how late she stays: hardly any weather keeps her indoors."

One day the west wind came full-breathed over land and sea, and Katipah was among the first on the beach to send up her messenger with word to Gamma-gata of the thing for which she prayed. "Gamma-gata," she sighed, "the voice of Bimsha afflicts me daily; my heart is bruised by the mockery she casts at me. Did I not love thee under the plum-tree, Gamma-gata? Ask of Heaven, therefore, that a child may be born to me—ever so small let it be—and Bimsha will become dumb. Gamma-gata, it is a very little thing that I am asking!"

All day long she let her kite go farther up into the sky than all the other kites. Overhead the wind sang in their strings like bees, or like the thin cry of very small children; but Katipah's was so far away she could scarcely see it against the blue. "Gamma-gata," she cried; till the twilight drew sea and land together, and she was left alone.

Then she called down her kite sadly; hand over hand she drew it by the cord, till she saw it fluttering over her head like a great moth searching for a flower in the gloom. "Wahoo! wahoo!" she could hear the wind crying through its strings like the wailing of a very small child.

It had become so dark that Katipah hardly knew what the kite had brought her till she touched the tiny warm limbs that lay cradled among the strings that netted the frame to its cord. Full of wonder and delight, she lifted the windling out of its nest, and laid it in her bosom. Then she slung her kite across her shoulder, and ran home, laughing and crying for joy and triumph to think that all Bimsha's mockery must now be at an end.

So, quite early the next morning, Katipah sat herself down very demurely in the doorway, with her child hidden in the folds of her gown, and waited for Bimsha's evil eye to look out upon her happiness.

She had not long to wait. Bimsha came out of her door, and looking across to Katipah, cried, "Well, Katipah, and where is your fine husband today?"

"My husband is gone out," said Katipah, "but if you care to look you can see my baby. It is ever so much more beautiful than yours."

Bimsha, when she heard that, turned green and yellow with envy; and there, plain to see, was Katipah holding up to view the most beautiful babe that ever gave the sunlight a good excuse for visiting this wicked earth. The mere sight of so much innocent beauty and happiness gave Bimsha a shock from which it took her three weeks to recover. After that she would sit at her window and for pure envy keep watch to see Katipah and the child playing together—the child which was so much more beautiful and well-behaved than her own.

As for Katipah, she was so happy now that the sorrow of waiting for her husband's return grew small. Day by day the west wind blew softly, and she knew that Gamma-gata was there, keeping watch over her and her child.

Every day she would say to the little one, "Come, my plump-petal, my wind-flower, I will send thee up to thy father that he may see how fat thou art getting, and be proud of thee!" And going down to the shore, she would lay the child among the strings of her kite and send it up to where Gamma-gata blew a wide breath over sea and land. As it went she would hear the child crow with joy at being so uplifted from earth, and laughing to herself, she would think, "When he sees his child so patterned after his own heart, Gamma-gata will be too proud to remain long away from me."

When she drew the child back to her out of the sky, she covered it with caresses, crying, "Oh, my wind-blown one, my cloudlet, my sky-blossom, my little piece out of heaven, hast thou seen thy father, and has he told thee that he loves me?" And the child would crow with mysterious delight, being too young to tell anything it knew in words.

Bimsha, out of her window, watched and saw all this, not comprehending it: and in her evil heart a wish grew up that she might by some means put an end to all Katipah's happiness. So one day towards evening, when Katipah, alone upon the shore, had let her kite and her little one go up to the fleecy edges of a cloud through which the golden sunlight was streaming, Bimsha came softly behind and with a sharp knife cut the string by which alone the kite was held from falling.

"Oh, silly Bimsha!" cried Katipah, "what have you done that for?"

Up in the air the kite made a far plunge forward, fluttered and stumbled in its course, and came shooting headlong to earth. "Oh dear!" cried Katipah, "if my beautiful little kite gets torn, Bimsha, that will be your fault!"

When the kite fell, it lay unhurt on one of the soft sandhills that ringed the bay; but no sign of the child was to be seen. Katipah was laughing when she picked up her kite and ran home. And Bimsha thought, "Is it witchcraft, or did the child fall into the sea?"

In the night the West Wind came and tapped at Katipah's window; and rising from her bed, she heard Gamma-gata's voice calling tenderly to her. When she opened the window to the blindness of the black night, he kissed her, and putting the little one in her arms, said, "Wait only a little while longer, Katipah, and I will come again to you. Already you are learning to be brave."

In the morning Bimsha looked out, and there sat Katipah in her own doorway, with the child safe and sound in her arms. And, plain to see, he had on a beautiful golden coat and little silver wings were fastened to his feet, and his head was garnished with a wreath of flowers the like of which were never seen on earth. He was like a child of noble birth and fortune, and the small motherly face of Katipah shone with pride and happiness as she nursed him.

"Where did you steal those things?" asked Bimsha, "and how did that child come back? I thought he had fallen into the sea and been drowned."

"Ah!" answered Katipah slyly, "he was up in the clouds when the kite left him, and he came down with the rain last night. It is nothing wonderful. You were foolish, Bimsha, if you thought that to fall into the clouds would do the child any harm. Up there you can have no idea how beautiful it is—such fields of gold, such wonderful gardens, such flowers and fruits: it is from there that all the beauty and wealth of the world must come. See all that he has brought with him! and it is all your doing, because you cut the cord of my kite. Oh, clever Bimsha!"

As soon as Bimsha heard that, she ran and got a big kite, and fastening her own child into the strings, started it to fly. "Do not think," cried the envious woman, "that you are the only one whose child is to be clothed in gold! My child is as good as yours any day; wait, and you shall see!"

So presently, when the kite was well up into the clouds, as Katipah's kite had been, she cut the cord, thinking surely that the same fortune would be for her as had been for Katipah. But instead of that, all at once the kite fell headlong to earth, child and all; and when she ran to pick him up, Bimsha found that her son's life had fallen forfeit to her own enviousness and folly.

The wicked woman went green and purple with jealousy and range; and running to the chief magistrate, she told him that while she was flying a kite with her child fastened to its back, Katipah had come and cut the string, so that by her doing the child was now dead.

When the magistrate heard that, he sent and caused Katipah to be thrown into prison, and told her that the next day she should certainly be put to death.

Katipah went meekly, carrying her little son in one hand and her blue-and-green kite in the other, for that had become so dear to her she could not now part from it. And all the way to prison Bimsha followed, mocking her, and asking, "Tell us, Katipah, where is your fine husband now?"

64

In the night the West Wind came and tapped at the prison window, and called tenderly, "Katipah, Katipah, are you there?" And when Katipah got up from her bed of straw and looked out, there was Gamma-gata once more, the beautiful youth whom she loved and had been wedded to, and had heard but had not seen since.

Gamma-gata reached his hands through the bars and put them round her face. "Katipah," he said, "you have become brave: you are fit now to become the wife of the West Wind. Tomorrow you shall travel with me all over the world; you shall not stay in one land any more. Now give me our son; for a little while I must take him from you. To prove your courage you must find your own way out of this trouble which you have got into through making a fool of Bimsha." So Katipah gave him the child through the bars of her prison window, and when he was gone lay down and slept till it became light.

In the morning the chief magistrate and Bimsha, together with the whole populace, came to Katipah's cell to see her led out to death. And when it was found that her child had disappeared, "She is a witch!" they cried; "she has eaten it!" And the chief magistrate said that, being a witch, instead of hanging she was to be burned.

"I have not eaten my child, and I am no witch," said Katipah, as, taking with her her blue-and-green kite she trotted out to the place of execution. When she was come to the appointed spot she said to the chief magistrate, "To every criminal it is permitted to plead in defence of himself; but because I am innocent, am I not also allowed to plead?" The magistrate told her she might speak if she had anything to say.

"All I ask," said Katipah, "is that I may be allowed once more to fly my blue-and-green kite as I used to do in the days when I was happy; and I will show you soon that I am not guilty of what is laid to my charge. It is a very little thing that I ask."

So the magistrate gave her leave; and there before all the people she sent up her kite till it flew high over the roofs of the town. Gently the West Wind took it and blew it away towards the sea. "Oh, Gamma-gata," she whispered softly, "hear me now, for I am not afraid."

The wind blew hard upon the kite, and pulled as though to catch it away, so Katipah twisted the cord once or twice round her waist that she might keep the safer hold over it. Then she said to the chief magistrate and to all the people that were assembled: "I am innocent of all that is charged against me; for, first, it was that wicked Bimsha herself who killed her own child."

"Prove it!" cried the magistrate.

"I cannot," replied Katipah.

"Then you must die!" said the magistrate.

"In the second place," went on Katipah, "I did not eat my own child."

"Prove it!" cried the chief magistrate again.

"I will," said Katipah; "O Gamma-gata, it is a very little thing that I ask."

Down the string of the kite, first a mere speck against the sky, then larger till plain for all to see came the missing one, slithering and sliding, with his golden coat, and the little silver wings tied to his ankles, and handfuls of flowers which he threw into his mother's face as he came. "Oh! cruel chief magistrate," cried Katipah, receiving the babe in her arms, "does it seem that I have eaten him?"

"You are a witch!" said the chief magistrate, "or how do you come to have a child that disappears and comes again from nowhere! It is not possible to permit such things to be:

you and your child shall both be burned together!"

Katipah drew softly upon the kite-string. "Oh, Gamma-gata," she cried, "lift me up now very high, and I will not be afraid!"

Then suddenly, before all eyes, Katipah was lifted up by the cord of the kite which she had wound about her waist; right up from the earth she was lifted till her feet rested above the heads of the people.

Katipah, with her babe in her arms, swung softly through the air, out of reach of the hands stretched up to catch her, and addressed the populace in these words:

"Oh, cruel people, who will not believe innocence when it speaks, you must believe me now! I am the wife of the West Wind—of Gamma-gata, the beautiful, the bearer of fine weather, who also brings back the wings that fly till the winter is over. Is it well, do you think, to be at war with the West Wind?

"Ah, foolish ones, I go now, for Gamma-gata calls me, and I am no longer afraid: I go to travel in many lands, whither he carries me, and it will be long before I return here. Many dark days are coming to you, when you shall not feel the west wind, the bearer of fine weather, blowing over you from land to sea; nor shall you see the blossoms open white over the hills, nor feel the earth grow warm as the summer comes in, because the bringer of fair weather is angry with you for the foolishness which you have done. But when at last the west wind returns to you, remember that Katipah the poor and unprofitable one, is Gamma-gata's wife, and that she has remembered, and has prayed for you."

And so saying, Katipah threw open her arms and let go the cord of the kite which held her safe. "Oh, Gamma-gata," she cried, "I do not see your eyes, but I am not afraid!" And at that, even while she seemed upon the point of falling to destruction, there flashed into sight a fair youth with dark hair and garments full of a storm of flying petals, who, catching up Katipah and her child in his arms, laughed scorn upon those below, and roaring over the roofs of the town, vanished away seawards.

When a chief magistrate and his people, after flagrant wrong-doing, become thoroughly cowed and frightened, they are apt also to be cruel. Poor Bimsha!

The Moon-flower

RINCESS Berenice sat by a window of her father's palace, looking out of the Moon. In her hand she held a great white pearl, and smiled, for it was her mother's birthday gift. The chamber in which she sat was of pure silver, and in the floor was a small window by which she could see out of the Moon and right down on to the Earth, where the moonbeams were going. There it lay like a great green emerald; and wherever the clouds parted to let the moonbeams go through, she could see the tops of trees, and broad fields with streams running by.

"Yonder is the land of the coloured stones," she said to herself, "that the merchants go down the moonbeams and bring home and sell." And as she bent lower and lower and gazed with curious eyes, the great pearl rolled from her hand and fell out of the Moon, and went slipping and sliding down a moonbeam, never stopping till it got to the Earth.

"My mother's pearl!" cried the Princess, "the most beautiful of all her pearls that she gave me. I must run down and bring it back; for if I wait it will be lost. And as tonight is the full-moon down there upon Earth, I can return before anyone finds out that I am gone."

The Earth was sparkling a brighter green under the approach of night. "Oh, land of the coloured stones!" cried the Princess; and, slipping through the window, she stepped out of the Moon, and went running down the same moonbeam by which the pearl had fallen.

Night came; and the Earth and the Moon lay looking at each other in the midst of heaven, like an emerald and a pearl; but through the palace, and within, over all its gardens and terraces there began to be callings on the Princess Berenice; and presently there were heart-searchings and fear, for they found the empty room with its open window: and the Princess Berenice was not there.

Now, not long before this, upon our own Earth there had lived and died a King who had four sons, but only three kingdoms. So when he came to die he gave to each of his three eldest sons a kingdom apiece; but to the youngest, having nothing else left to give, he gave only a pair of travelling shoes, and said: "Wear these, and some day they will take you to fortune!"

So, when the King was dead, the young Prince wore the shoes night and day, hoping that some time or another they would take him to fortune. His brothers laughed at him, and said: "Our father was wise to play those old shoes off upon you! If it had been either of us we would have gone and bought ourselves an army and fought for a just share in the inheritance. But you seem pleased, so we ought to be."

Now one day the Prince went out hunting in the forest, and there, having become separated from all his friends, he thoroughly lost his way. Wherever he turned the wood seemed to grow denser, the thickets higher, and the solitude more than he ever remembered before. Night came on, and, there being nothing else that he could do, he lay down and wrapped himself in his cloak and slept.

When he awoke it was day, but the woods were as still as death; no bird sang, and not a cricket chirped among the grass. As he sat up he noticed that the shoe was gone from his left foot, nor could he see it anywhere near. "'Tis the half of my inheritance gone!" he said to himself, and got up to search about him. But still no shoe could he find. At last he gave up the search as useless, and set off walking without it. Then as it seemed to him so ridiculous to go limping along with only one shoe on, he took off the remaining one, and threw it away, saying: "Go, stupid, and find your fellow!"

To the Prince's great astonishment, it set off at a rapid pace through the wood, all of its own accord. The Prince, barefoot except for his stockings, began to run after it.

Presently he found that he was losing his breath. "Hie, hie!" he called out, "not quite so fast, little leather-skins!" But the shoe paid him no heed and went on as before. It skipped through the grass and brushwood, as if a young girl's foot were dancing inside it; and whenever it came to a fallen tree, or a boulder of rock it was up and over with a jump like a grasshopper.

Before long the Prince's stockings were nothing but holes and tatters; as he ran they fluttered from his legs like ribbons. He had lost his hat, and his cloak was torn into patterns, and he felt from head to foot like a house all doors and windows. He was almost on his last gasp when he saw that the shoe was making straight for a strange little house of green bronze, shut in by a high wall, and showing no windows; and in the middle of the wall was a bronze door shut fast. As he came near he found that outside, on the doorstep, stood his other shoe as if waiting to be let in. "So it was worth running for!" thought he; and then, putting on both shoes again, he began knocking at the door.

As he knocked the door opened. It opened in such a curious way, flat down like a swing-bridge or like the lid of a box. For some time he was half afraid to walk in on the top of it. Presently, however, he summoned up his courage and stepped across it.

The door closed behind him like a trap, and he found

himself in a beautiful house; all its walls were hung with gold and precious stones, but everywhere was the emptiness and the silence of death.

He went from room to room seeking for any that lived there, but could see no one. In one place he found thrown down a fan of white feathers and pearl; and in another flowers, fresh plucked, lying close by a cushion dinted and hollowed, as though the weight of a head or arm had rested there. But beyond these there was no sign of a living thing to be found.

Through the windows he saw deep bowery gardens hemmed in by high walls, within which grew flowers of the loveliest kinds. All the paths were of smooth grass, and everywhere were the traces of gentle handiwork; but still not a soul was to be seen.

It seemed to the Prince now and then that there was something in the garden which moved, distinct from the flowers, and shifting with a will of its own. Though the sun shone full down, casting clear shadows across the lawns, this that he saw was altogether misty and faint. Now it seemed like a feather blown to and fro in the wind, and now like broken gossamer threads, or like filmy edges of clouds melting away in the heat. Where it went the flowers moved as though to make way for it, swaying apart and falling together again as it passed.

The Prince watched and watched. He tired his eyes with watching, yet he could see no more; and no way could he find to the garden, for all the doors leading to it were locked fast and barred.

There was another strange thing he noticed which seemed to him to have no meaning. All over the garden, between the trees and the sky, was stretched a silver net, so fine that it showed only as a faint film against the blue; but a net for all that. Here and there, the light of the sun catching it, hung sparkling in its silver meshes. It was like the net that a gardener throws over strawberry beds or currant bushes to keep off the birds from the fruit. So was it with this net; through it no bird could enter the garden, and no bird that was in the garden could leave it.

All day the Prince had these two things before his eyes to wonder about, till the sun went down and it began to get dusk.

At the moment when the sun sank below the earth there was a sound of opening doors all over the house. The Prince ran and found one of the doors leading into the garden wide open, and through it he could see the stir of leaves, and the deep colours of the flowers growing deeper in the dusk; only the evening primroses were lighting their soft lamps.

From a distant part of the garden came the sound of falling water, and a voice singing. As he approached he saw something shining against the dark leaves higher than the heads of the flowers; and before he well knew what he saw, he found before his eyes the most lovely woman that the mind of man could believe in.

In her hand hung a watering-can, with the water falling from it in sprays on to the flower beds beneath. Her head was bent far down, yet how she looked slender and tall! She was very pale, yet a soft light seemed to grow from her, the light of a new moon upon a twilight sky. And now the Prince heard clearly the sweet voice, and the words that she was singing:

> "Listen, listen, listen,
>   O heart of the sea!
> I am the Pearl of pearls
> I am the Mother of pearls,
>   And the Mother of thee.

Glisten, glisten, glisten,
  O bed of the sea!
Lost is the Pearl of pearls,
And all the divers for pearls
  Are drowning for me."

He stood enchanted to hear her; but the words of the song ended suddenly in a deep sigh. The singer lifted her head; her eyes moved like grey moths in the dusk, amid the whiteness of her face. At sight of him they grew still and large, widening with a quiet wonder. Then the beautiful face broke into smiles, and the Princess stretched out her hands to him and laughed.

"Have you come," she said, "to set me free?"

"To set you free?" asked the Prince.

"I am a prisoner," she told him.

"Alas, then!" answered the Prince, "I am a prisoner also, and can free no one; but were I now free to go wherever I would, I should be a prisoner still, for I have seen the face of the loveliest heart on earth!"

"Alas!" she sighed, "and can you not set me free?"

"Tell me," he said, "what makes you a prisoner here?"

She pointed to the net over their heads, to the walls that stood on all sides of them, and to the ground beneath their feet. "That," she said, "and that, and this."

"Who are you?" he asked, "and where do you come from? and whose power is it that now holds you captive?"

She led him on to a terrace, from which they could see out towards the west; and there lay the new Moon, low down in the sky. "Yonder," she said, pointing to it, "is my home!" She wept. "Shall I ever return to it?"

The Prince, gazing at her in wonder, cried, "Are you one of a Fairy race?"

"No, oh, no!" she sighed. "I am but mortal like yourself; only my home is there, while yours is here. We, who dwell in the Moon, are as you are, but the sun has greater power over us; the light of it falling on us makes us pale and unsubstantial, so that we weigh not so much as a gossamer and become transparent as thin fleeces of cloud. Then we can go where you cannot go, treading the light as it flies; but at sunset we regain our strength, and our bodies come to us again; and we are as you see me now—no different from yourselves, the inhabitants of the Earth."

"Tell me," said the Prince, "of yourself, and the dwellers in the Moon! Is it not cold there, and barren?"

She answered smiling, for the memory of her home was sweet to her, "Outside, the Moon is cold and barren; but within it is very warm and rich and fertile; more beautiful than any place I have seen on Earth. It is there we live; and we have flocks, and herds, and woods, and rivers, and harbours, and seas. Also we have great cities built inside the Moon's crust, for the Moon is a great hollow shell, and we walk upon its inner surface and are warm. The sunlight comes to us through craters and clefts in the ground; and the beams of it are like solid pillars of gold that quiver and sway as they shoot upwards into the opal twilight of our world; and the shine and the warmth of it come to us, and colour the air above our heads; but we are safe from its full light falling on us, for the ground is between us and it. Only when we pass through to the outer side do we become pale and faint, a mere whisper of our former selves. And then we are so light that if we step upon a moonbeam it will bear our weight; and the moonbeam carries us swiftly as its own light travels, till it reaches the Earth: so we come. But to return there is another way."

And when the Prince asked her, she told him of the other

way back into the Moon.

"When we wish to return," she went on, "for the falling light of a moonbeam cannot carry us back, we must go where there is a pool of still water and wait for the reflection of the Moon to fall on it; and when the Moon is full, and throws its image into the water, then we dive down, and with our lips touch the reflection of its face, crying, 'Open, open to me, for I am a Moon-child!' And the Moon will open her face like a door of pearl, and let us pass in; and when she draws her reflection out of the pool, we find ourselves once again among our own people and in our own land. Many of us have so come and so returned," she sighed deeply, "but I fear that I shall never again return."

Then the Prince asked her further whose power it was that held her captive; and she told him how she had dropped the pearl that her mother had given her, and had come down seeking it. Then she said, "In the Moon we have many jewels, for we have opals and onyxes, and pearls and moonstones, but we have no rubies, or emeralds, or sapphires, or stones of a single colour, such as you have. Therefore, we have a passion for these things, and our merchants come down and bring them back to us at a great price.

"Now it chanced that in my search I came upon a gnome who had dealings with our merchants and had many jewels to sell, and he, seeming to be kind, helped me until my pearl was found. Then he took me to see his own treasures; and, alas, while my eyes were feasting on the colours of the stones he showed to me, my poor beauty inflamed the avarice of his evil heart, and the desire to have me for his wife became great. So when I asked him the price of his jewels, he vowed that the only price at which he would let them go was that of my own hand in marriage. Alas, I am young and innocent, and without subtlety, nor did I know how great was his power

and wickedness. As I laughed at his request his face grew dark with rage, and I saw that I had incurred the undying enmity of his cruel heart. And now for a whole year he has held me in his enchantment, striving to break me to his will by the length and weariness of my captivity; and lest search or any help should come for me from my father's people, he has covered me in with a net, and surrounded me with walls; and here there is no pool into which the full Moon may fall, and at the mere touch of my lips upon its face, open and draw me free from my enchantment, and back into the heart of my own land. Only yonder, in the corner of the garden is a deep well, where the Moon never shines; so there is no way here left for me by which I may get free."

"Does not the gnome ever come to see you in your captivity?" asked the Prince. "If so, I may by some means be able to entrap him, and force him to let you go."

"Twice in the year he has visited me," answered the Princess. "He comes up out of the ground in the form of a Red Mole; but he looks at me wickedly and cunningly with the eyes of a man, seeming to say, 'Will you have me yet?' And when I shake my head he burrows under again, and is gone till another six months shall be past."

The Prince thought for a while and said, "I do not know whether I have the power or the wit to make you free; if love only were needed for the work, tomorrow would see you as free as a bird."

The Princess, between smiles and sighs, said, "I have been most lonely here; already you make my imprisonment seem less." Then she led him within doors, from room to room, showing him the splendours of her prison. Wherever they went, out of the floor before them rose burning jewels that hung hovering over their heads to light them as they passed; and when she struck her hands together, up from the ground rose a table covered with fruit and dainties of all sorts; and when she and the Prince had eaten, she clapped her hands again, and they disappeared by the same way that they had come.

The Prince was struck with admiration at the delicacy of these marvels. "When I think of the Red Mole, they sicken me!" said the Moon-Princess. The good youth used all his arts to cheer her, promising to devote himself, and if need be his life, to the task of setting her free. And now and then she laughed and was almost merry again, forgetting the walls that still held her spell-bound from her own people and her own land.

She showed the Prince a chamber where he might sleep; and so soft and warm was the couch after his last hard night on the ground, that it was full day before he awoke. The Princess Berenice appeared before him misty and faint, for the sunlight threw a veil upon her beauty; but still as he looked at her he did not love her less, and it still seemed to him that hers was the face of the loveliest heart on Earth.

All day he watched her drifting about the garden, seeming to feed herself on the scent of the flowers. In the evening, when the sun set, her body grew strong and her face shone out to him like the new Moon upon a twilight sky.

Then he drew water for her from the well, and watched her as she watered the flowers which were her only delight. Presently he said, "There is much water in the well, for the rope goes down into it many fathoms; and yet I find no bottom."

"Yes," answered the Princess, "I doubt not that the well is deep."

"Before many days are over," said the Prince, "the well shall become a pool."

The Princess wondered to hear him. "Is there," he went on, "no such thing as a spade for me to dig with?" Then she led him to a shed, where lay all the needed implements for gardening. So his eyes brightened, while he cried, "O, beautiful Princess Berenice, as I love you, before many weeks are over you shall be free!"

The next morning he arose very early, and in the centre of the garden, where the ground hollowed somewhat, he marked out a space and set to work to dig.

All day the Princess went to and fro, faint and pale as a mist, watching him at his work. At dusk her beauty shone full upon him, and she said, "What is this that you are doing?" He answered, "What I am making shall presently become a pool; then when the pool is full, and the full Moon comes and shines on it, you shall go down into the water, and shall kiss the face of its reflection with your lips, and be free from your enchantment."

Princess Berenice looked long at him, and her eyes clung to his like soft moths in the gloom. "But you?" she said, "You are no Moon-child, and this will never set you free."

"Ever since I saw you," said the Prince, "I have not thought of freedom; my dearest wish is but to set you free."

The Princess gave him her hand. "And mine," she said, "my dearest wish henceforth is to set you free also. Yet I know but one way, and I cannot name it." She smiled tenderly on him, and bowed her face into the shadow of her hair.

The Prince caught her in his arms, "One way is my way!" he cried. "Your way," she said, "is my way." Then, when he had finished kissing her, she said, "Look, on my finger is a ring; this ring is for him to whom I give myself in marriage. Surely, it opens to him the heart of my own people, and he becomes one of us, a child of the Moon." She showed him an opal ring, full of fires. "If your way is my way," she said, "draw this off my finger, and put it upon your own, and take me to be your wife!"

So the Prince drew off the ring from her finger, and set it

upon his own; and as he did so he felt indeed the heart of the Moon-people become his own, and the love of the Moon strike root in him. Yet did the love of the Earth remain his as well, making it seem as if all the love in his heart had but doubled itself.

So he and the most beautiful Berenice were married there by the light of the new Moon, and all thought of sorrow or danger from the encirclement that bound them was lost in their great joy.

During the whole of the next day the Prince went on with his digging, making a broad shallow in the ground. "Before the full Moon comes," he said, "I will make it deep." And he worked on, refusing to take any rest.

The Princess loved him more and more as she watched him; and his love for her daily increased, for every day, while the Moon grew full, her beauty shone in greater perfection and splendour. "Here," she said to him, "the coming of the full Moon is like the coming of Spring to me: I feel it in my blood. After the full Moon my beauty will wane and grow paler. But in my own land I do not feel these changes, for there it is always the full Moon." The Prince answered her, "To me your beauty, though it grows more, will not ever grow less."

At last, on the day before that of the full Moon, the pit which he had dug was broad and deep; then he began to fill it with water from the well. "Tomorrow," he said to his wife, when the pool was nearly full, as she came and stood by his side at sunset in the full blaze of her beauty, "tomorrow we shall be free; and you will carry me away with you into your own land."

"I do not know," said the Princess; "I begin to be afraid!" and she sighed heavily. "Any day the Red Mole may come: one day is not too soon for him to be here."

'But why need you fear him now?" asked the Prince. "Since you are married to me, you cannot be married to him."

"As to that," said she, "I fear that to have outwitted him will but make his malice all the greater against us!" Then she walked softly among the moonbeams, bathing her hands in them, and letting them fall upon the loveliness of her face; and as she stood in their light, tears rained down out of her eyes.

In the morning it seemed as if her happiness had returned. The Prince, as he toiled under the blazing sun, carrying water from the well to the pool, felt her moving by his side, and heard her light shadowy laughter when, just before sunset, the water flowed level to the pool's brink. And when dusk rose out of the grass, there she stood glowing with the full Moon of her beauty and leaning in all the light of her loveliness towards him.

The happy night drew round them; out of the East came the glow of the full Moon as it rose; soon, soon it would cross the tops of the trees and rest its face upon the quiet waters of the pool. They clung in each other's arms, entranced. "My beautiful," said the Prince, "shall we not take to your mother some of those jewels she loves—the green, and the red, and the blue, and the pearl which was hers, the quest of which has cost you so much?" He ran into one of the jewelled chambers where lay the pearl, and caught from the walls the largest stones he could find. Quickly he went and returned, for the Moon was now fast cresting the avenues of the garden. He came bearing the jewels in his hands.

Princess Berenice stood no longer by the brink of the pool, though therein lay the image of the Moon's face, a circle of pale gold upon the water. "Berenice," called the Prince, and ran through the garden searching for her. "Berenice!" he cried by the well; but she was not there. "Berenice!" His voice grew trembling and weak, and quick fear took hold of him. "O, my beautiful, my beloved, where are you?"

Only the silence stood up to answer him. Under his feet ran a Red Mole.

It scampered across the grass, and disappeared through a burrow in the ground. Then the Prince knew that the worst had surely come, and that his Princess had been taken away from him. Where she was he could not know; within her former prison she was nowhere to be seen.

All night the Prince lay weeping by the brink of the pool, where she had last stood before his sight; the print of her dear feet still lay on the lawn where she had stayed waiting with him so long. "O, miserable wretch that I am!" he cried, kissing the trodden grass. "Now never again may I hope to behold you, or hear your dear voice!"

All the day following he wandered like a ghost from place to place, filling the empty garden with memories of her presence, and sighing over and over again the music of her name. All the flowers glowed round him in their accustomed beauty; new buds came into life, and full blooms broke and fell; not a thing seemed to sorrow for her loss except himself. As for the flowers, he paid them little heed.

In his sleep that night a dream came to him, a dream as of something that whispered and laughed in his ear. Over and over again it seemed to be saying, "The Red Mole came, and the full Moon came, and the Princess jumped down into the water!" Then his heart knocked so loud for joy that he started awake, and saw the Red Mole scuffling away to its burrow in the ground.

Then he feared that the dream was but a thing devised to cheat his fancy, and get rid of him by making him go away and search for his Princess in the land of the Moon, by the way that she had told him. But he thought to himself, "If the Red Mole wants so much to get me away, it means that my beloved is somewhere near at hand. Is she in the well?" he began wondering; and as soon as it was light he went to where lay the well in its corner under the shadow of the wall. But though he searched long and diligently, there was no trace of her that he could find.

Yet every time he came near to the well sorrow seemed to take hold of him, and, mixed with it, a kind of joy, as though indeed the heart of his beloved beat in this place. Near to the well stood a tall flower with bowed head. It seemed to him the only one in the whole garden that had any share in his sorrow: he wondered if the flower had grown up to mark the sad place of her burial.

"O, my beloved Berenice, art thou near me now?" he murmured, heart-broken, one day as he passed by: then it seemed to him that all at once the flower stirred. He turned to look at it; it was like a sunflower, but white even to its centre, and its head kept drooping as if for pure grief. "Berenice, Berenice!" he wept, passing it.

At dusk he returned again; and now the flower's head was lifted up, and shone with a strange lustre. The Prince, as he went by on his way to the well, saw the flower turn its head, bending its face ever towards where he was. Then grief and joy stirred in his heart. "The flower knows where she is!" he said.

So he bent, whispering, "Where, then, is Berenice?" and the flower lifted its head, and hung quite still, looking at him.

Then the Prince whispered again, "The Red Mole came, and the full Moon came, and the Princess jumped down into the water?"

But the flower swayed its head from side to side, and the

Prince found that it had answered "No."

Then he had it in his mind to ask of it further things; but, as he was about to speak, he beheld its face all brimming over with tears, that suddenly broke and fell down in a shower over its leaves.

At that his heart leaped, and his voice choked as he cried, "Art *thou* my beloved, my Berenice?" And all at once the flower swayed down, and leaned, and fell weeping against his breast.

So at last he knew! And joy and grief struggled together in him for mastery.

All that night he knelt with the flower's head upon his heart, stroking its soft leaves, and letting it rest between his hands; till, towards dawn, it seemed to him that peace was upon it and sleep.

All through the day it hung faint upon its stem; but when evening came it lifted its head and shone in Moon-like beauty; and so deep for it was the Prince's love and compassion that he could hardly bear to be absent from its side one moment of the day or night.

And, when he was very weary, he lay down under its shadow to sleep; and the Moon-flower bent down and rested its head upon his face.

All night long in dreams Berenice came back to him. He seemed to hear how the Red Mole had come, and changed her to a rooted shape, lest the full Moon in the water should carry her away from him back into her own land. Yet it was only a dream, and the Prince could learn nothing there of the way by which he might set her free.

A month went by, and he said to his Flower, "Tonight is the night of the full Moon: now, if I drew you from the ground, and carried you down, and called for the Moon's face to open to us, would you not be free from the enchant-

ment, when you were come again to your own people?" But the Moon-flower shook its head, as if to bid him still wait and watch patiently.

Now, as the Prince came and went day by day, he began to notice that the Moon-flower had its roots in a small green mound, no bigger than a mole-hill; and he thought to himself, "surely that mound was not there at first: the Red Mole must be down below at work!" So he watched it from day to day; and at last he knew for certain that, as time went on, the mound grew larger.

Month by month the mound upon which the Moon-flower had root increased in size; yet the Flower thrived, and its beauty shone brighter as each full Moon approached, so that at last the Prince's fear lest the Red Mole were working mischief against its life, passed away.

Once, on the night of a full Moon, as the Prince lay with his head upon Earth, and the Moon-flower bowed over his face, he heard under the mound a peal of silvery laughter; and at the sound of it the Moon-flower started, and stood erect, and a stir of delight seemed to take hold of its leaves. Again the laughter came, and the soft earth moved at the sound of it.

The Prince started up, and ran and fetched a spade, and struck it down under the loose soil of the mound. When he lifted up the earth, out sprang a tiny child like a lobe of quicksilver, laughing merrily with its first leap into the light. But even then its laughter changed into a cry; for out after it darted the Red Mole, with fury in its whiskers, and wrath flashing out of its eyes.

The quicksilver child sprang away, darting swiftly over the grass towards the margin of the pool. There lay the full Moon's image upon the clear stillness of the water; and the child leapt down the bank, and laughed as it sprang safely away. Then there followed a tiny splash; and the Prince, amid the rings upon the water's surface, saw, like a door of pearl, the Moon's face open and close again. And the Red Mole went down into the earth gnashing its teeth for rage.

The Prince ran back to the Moon-flower, and found it bent forward and trembling with fear. Then he drew its head towards his heart, and whispered "The Red Mole came, and the full Moon came, and the silver child jumped down into the water!" And at that the Flower lifted its head and began clapping its leaves for joy.

A month went by, and the green mound had disappeared from beneath the Moon-flower's roots; and still every night the Prince lay down under the shadow of its leaves; and the Flower bent over him, and laid its head against his face.

As he lay so, one night, and watched the full Moon travelling high overhead, he saw a shadow begin to cross over it; and he knew that it was the eclipse, which is the shadow of the Earth passing over the face of the Moon; then he rose softly, leaving the Moon-flower asleep, and went and stood by the brink of the pool.

Up in the Moon the silver child felt the shadow of the Earth fall upon the face of the Moon; and he came and touched the Earth's shadow with his lips, crying, "Open, open to me, for I am an Earth-child!" Then the Earth's shadow that was upon the Moon opened, and the silver child sprang through.

The Prince, watching the veiled image of the Moon's face in the water, saw the Earth's shadow open like a door, so that for an instant the brightness of the Moon shone through, and out sprang the quicksilver child, up to the surface of the pool.

He leapt laughing up the bank, and went running over the grass to where the Moon-flower was standing. He reached up his arms, and caught the Flower by the head.

"O mother, mother, mother!" he cried as he kissed it.

And at the touch of his lips the Moon-flower opened and changed, growing wondrously tall and fair; and the flower turned into a face, and the leaves disappeared, till it was the beautiful Princess Berenice herself, who stooped down and took the quicksilver child up into her arms.

She cried, fondling him, "Did they give you your name?"

And the child laughed. "They call me Gammelyn," he said.

The Prince caught them both together in his arms. "Come, come!" he shouted and laughed, "for yonder is the full Moon waiting for us!" And, lifting them up, he ran with them to the borders of the pool.

And the Red Mole came, and the full Moon came; and the Prince, and the Princess, and the silver child jumped down into the water.

Then the Prince laid his lips against the reflection of the Earth's shadow, crying, "Open, open to me, for I am a child of the Earth!" And the shadow opened like a door to let them pass through. Then they pressed their lips against the reflection of the Moon's face crying, "Open, open to us, for we are Moon-children!" And the Moon opened her face like a door of pearl, so that they sprang through together, and were safe.

And when the Moon drew its reflection out of the pool, they found themselves in the land of the Moon, in the silver chamber with the round window, in the palace of Princess Berenice's father.

Looking out through the window, down at the end of a long moonbeam they saw the Red Mole gnashing his whiskers for rage. Then the Prince took off his shoes, and threw them with all his might down the moonbeam at the Mole.

As the shoes fell, they went faster, and faster, and faster, till they came to earth; and they struck the Mole so hard upon the head that he died.

Now as for Gammelyn and the shoes we may hear of them again elsewhere; but as for the Prince and his beautiful Princess Berenice, the happiness in which they lived for the rest of their days is too great even to be told.

The Moon-stroke

N the hollow heart of an old tree a Jackdaw and his wife had made themselves a nest. As soon as the mother of his eggs had finished laying, she sat waiting patiently for something to come of it. One by one five mouths poked out of the shells, demanding to be fed; so for weeks the happy couple had to be continually in two places at once searching for food to satisfy them.

Presently the wings of the young ones grew strong; they could begin to fly about; and the parents found time for a return to pleasuring and curiosity-hunting. They began gathering in a wise assortment of broken glass and chips of platter to grace the corners of their dwelling. All but the youngest Jackdaw were enchanted with their unutterable beauty and value; they were never tired of quarrelling over the possession and arrangement of them.

"But what are they for?" asked the youngest, a perverse bird who kept himself apart from the rest, and took no share in their daily squabblings.

The mother-bird said: "They are beautiful, and what God intended for us: therefore they must be true. We may not see the use of them yet, but no doubt some day they will come true."

The little Jackdaw said: "Their corners scratch me when I want to go to sleep; they are far worse than crumbs in the bed. All the other birds do without them—why should not we?"

"That is what distinguishes us from the other birds!" replied the Janedaw, and thanked her stars that it was so.

"I wish we could sing!" sighed the littlest young Jackdaw.

"Babble, babble!" replied his mother angrily.

And then, as it was dinner-time, he forgot his grief, as they all said grace and fell-to.

One evening the old Jackdaw came home very late, carrying something that burned bright and green, like an evening star; all the nest shone where he set it down.

"What do you think of that for a discovery?" he said to the Janedaw.

"Think?" she said; "I can't. Some of it looks good to eat; but that fire-patch at the end would burn one's inside out."

Presently the Jackdaw family settled itself down to sleep; only the youngest one sat up and watched. Now he had seen something beautiful. Was it going to come true? Its light was like the song of the nightingale in the leaves overhead: it glowed, and throbbed, and grew strong, flooding the whole place where it lay.

Soon, in the silence, he heard a little wail of grief: "Why have they carried me away here," sighed the glow-worm, "out of the tender grass that loves the ground?"

The littlest Jackdaw listened with all his heart. Now something at last was going to become true, without scratching his legs and making him feel as though crumbs were in his bed.

A little winged thing came flying down to the green light, and two voices began crying together—the glow-worm and its mate.

"They have carried you away?"

"They have carried me away; up here I shall die!"

"I am too weak to lift you," said the one with wings; "you will stay here, and you will die!" Then they cried yet more.

"It seems to me," thought the Jackdaw, "that as soon as the beautiful becomes true, God does not intend it to be for us." He got up softly from among his brothers. I will carry you down," he said. And without more ado, he picked it up and carried it down out of the nest, and laid it in the long grass at the foot of the tree.

Overhead the nightingale sang, and the full moon shone; its rays struck down on the little Jackdaw's head.

For a bird that is not a nightingale to wake up and find its head unprotected under the rays of a full moon is serious: there and then he became moon-struck. He went back into bed; but he was no longer the same little Jackdaw. "Oh, I wish I could sing!" he thought; and not for hours could he get to sleep.

In the morning, when the family woke up, the beautiful and the true was gone. The father Jackdaw thought he must have swallowed it in his sleep.

"If you did," said his wife, "there'll be a smell of burnt feathers before long!"

But the littlest Jackdaw said, "It came true, and went away, because it was never intended for us."

Now some days after this the old Jackdaw again came carrying something that shone like an evening star—a little spike of gold with a burning emerald set in the end of it. "And what do you think of that?" said he to his wife.

"I daren't come near it," she answered, "for fear it should burn me!"

That night the little Jackdaw lay awake, while all the others slept, waiting to hear the green stone break out into sorrow, and to see if its winged mate would come seeking it. But after hours had gone, and nothing stirred or spoke, he slipped softly out of the nest, and went down to search for the poor little winged mate who must surely be about somewhere.

And now, truly, among the grasses and flowers he heard something sobbing and sighing; a little winged thing darted into sight and out again, searching the ground like a dragon-fly at quest. And all the time, amid the darting and humming of its wings, came sobbing and wringing of hands.

The young Jackdaw called: "Little wings, what have you lost? Is it not a spike with a green light at the end of it?"

"My wand, my wand!" cried the fairy, beside herself with grief. "Just about sunset I was asleep in an empty wren's nest, and when I woke up my wand was gone!"

Then the little Jackdaw, being moon-struck, and not knowing the value of things, flew up to the nest and brought back the fairy her wand.

"Oh!" she cried, "you have saved my life!" And she thanked the Jackdaw till he grew quite modest and shy.

"What is it for? What can you do with it?" he asked.

"With this," she answered, "I can make anything beautiful come true! I can give you whatever you ask; you have but to ask, and you shall have."

Then the little Jackdaw, being moon-struck, and not knowing the value of things, said, "Oh, if I could only sing like a nightingale!"

"You can!" said the fairy, waving her wand but once; and immediately something like a melodious sneeze flew into his head and set it shaking.

"Chiou! chiou! True-true-true-true! Jug! jug! Oh, beautiful! beautiful!" His beak went dabbling in the sweet sound, rippling it this way and that, spraying it abroad out of his blissful heart as a jewel throws out its fires.

The fairy was gone; but the little Jackdaw sprang up into the high elm, and sang on endlessly through the whole night.

At dawn he stopped, and looking down, there he saw the family getting ready for breakfast, and wondering what had become of him.

Just as they were saying grace he flew in, his little heart beating with joy over his new-found treasure. What a jewel of a voice he had: better than all the pieces of glass and chips of platter lying down there in the nest! As soon as the parent-birds had finished grace, he lifted his voice and thanked God that the thing he had wished for had become true.

None of them understood what he said, but they paid him plenty of attention. All his brothers and sisters put up their heads and giggled, as the young do when one of their number misbehaves.

"Don't make that noise!" said his mother; "it's not decent!"

"It's low!" said the father-bird.

The littlest young Jackdaw was overwhelmed with astonishment. When he tried to explain, his unseemly melodies led to his immediate expulsion from the family circle. Such noises, he was told, could only be made in private; when he had quite got over them he might come back—but not until.

He never got over them; so he never came back. For a few days he hid himself in different trees of the garden, and sang the praises of sorrow; but his family, though they comprehended him not, recognized his note, and came searching him with beak and claw, and drove him out so as not to have him near them committing such scandalous noises to the ears of the public.

"He lies in his throat!" said the old Jackdaw. "Everything he says he garbles. If he is our son he must have been hatched on the wrong side of the nest!"

After that, wherever he went, all the birds jeered at and persecuted him. Even the nightingales would not listen to his brotherly voice. They made fun of his black coat, and called him a Nonconformist without a conscience. "All this has come about," thought he, "because God never meant anything beautiful to come true."

One day a man who saw him and heard him singing, caught him, and took him round the world in a cage for show. The value of him was discovered. Great crowds came to see the little Jackdaw, and to hear him sing. He was described now as the "Amphabulous Philomel, or the Mongrel-Minstrel"; but it gave him no joy.

Before long he had become what we call tame—that is to say, his wings had been clipped; he was allowed out of his cage, because he could no longer fly away, and he sang when he was told, because he was whipped if he did not.

One day there was a great crowd round the travelling booth where he was on view: the showman had a new wonder which he was about to show to the people. He took the little Jackdaw out of his cage, and set him to perch upon his shoulder, while he busied himself over something which he was taking carefully out of ever so many boxes and coverings.

The Jackdaw's sad eye became attracted by a splendid scarf-pin that the showman wore—a gold pin set with a tiny emerald that burned like fire. The bird thought, "Now if only the beautiful could become true!"

And now the showman began holding up a small glass bottle for the crowd to stare into. The people were pushing this way and that to see what might be there.

At the bottom sat the little fairy, without her wand, weeping and beating her hands on the glass.

The showman was so proud he grew red in the face, and ran shouting up and down the plank, shaking and turning the bottle upside down now and then, so as to make the cabined fairy use her wings, and buzz like a fly against the glass.

The Jackdaw waggled unsteadily at his perch on the man's shoulder. "Look at him!" laughed someone in the crowd, "he's going to steal his master's scarf-pin."

"Ho, ho, ho!" shouted the showman. "See this bird now! See the marvellous mongrel nature of the beast! Who tells me he's only a nightingale painted black?"

The people laughed the more at that, for there was a fellow in the crowd looking sheepish. The Jackdaw had drawn out the scarf-pin, and held it gravely in its beak, looking sideways with cunning eyes. He was wishing hard. All the crowd laughed again.

Suddenly the showman's hand gave a jerk, the bottle slipped from his hold and fell, shivering itself upon the ground.

There was a buzz of wings—the fairy had escaped.

"The beautiful is coming true," thought the Jackdaw, as he yielded to the fairy her wand, and found, suddenly, that his wings were not clipped after all.

"What more can I do for you?" asked the fairy, as they flew away together. "You gave me back my wand; I have given you back your wings."

"I will not ask anything," said the little Jackdaw; "what God intends will come true."

"Let me take you up to the moon," said the fairy. "All the Jackdaws up there sing like nightingales."

"Why is that?" asked the little Jackdaw.

"Because they are all moon-struck," she answered.

"And what is it to be moon-struck?" he asked.

"Surely you should know, if anyone!" laughed the fairy. "To see things beautifully, and not as they are. On the moon you will be able to do that without any difficulty."

"Ah," said the little Jackdaw, "now I know at last that the beautiful is going to come true!"

Gammelyn, the Dressmaker

HERE was once upon a time a King's daughter who was about to be given in marriage to a great prince; and when the wedding-day was yet a long way off, the whole court began to concern itself as to how the bride was to be dressed. What she should wear, and how she should wear it, was the question debated by the King and his Court day and night, almost without interruption. Whatever it was to be, it must be splendid, without peer. Must it be silk, or velvet, or satin; should it be enriched with brocade, or with gems, or sewn thick with pearls?

But when they came to ask the Princess, she said, "I will have only a dress of beaten gold, light as gossamer, thin as bee's wing, soft as swan's-down."

Then the King, calling his chief goldsmith, told him to make for the Princess the dress of beaten gold. But the goldsmith knew no way how such a dress was to be made, and his answer to the King was, "Sire, the thing is not to be done."

Then the King grew very angry, for he said, "What a Princess can find it in her head to wish, some man must find it in his wits to accomplish." So he put the chief goldsmith in prison to think about it, and summoning all the goldsmiths in the kingdom, told them of the Princess's wish, that a dress should be made for her of beaten gold. But every one of the goldsmiths went down on his knees to the King, saying, "Sire,

the thing is not to be done." Thereupon the King clapped them all into prison, promising to cut off all their heads if in three weeks' time they had not put them together to some purpose and devised a plan for making such a dress as the Princess desired.

Now just then Gammelyn was passing through the country, and when he heard of all this, he felt very sorry for the goldsmiths, who had done nothing wrong, but had told honest truth about themselves to the King. So he set his bright wits to work, and at last said, "I think I can save the goldsmiths their heads, for I have found a way of making such a dress as this fine Princess desires."

Then he went to the King and said, "I have a way for making a dress of beaten gold."

"But," said the King, "have a care, for if you fail I shall assuredly cut off your head."

All the same Gammelyn took that risk willingly and set to work. And first he asked that the Princess would tell him what style of dress it should be; and the Princess said, "Beaten gold, light as gossamer, thin as bee's-wing, soft as swan's-down, and it must be made thus." So she showed him of what fashion sleeve, and bodice, and train should be. Then Gammelyn caused to be made (for he had a palace full of workers put under him) a most lovely dress, in the fashion the Princess had named, of white cambric closely woven; and the Princess came wondering at him, saying that it was to be only of beaten gold.

"You wait a while!" said Gammelyn, for he had no liking for the Princess. Then he asked the King for gold out of his treasury; but the King supplied him instead with gold from the stores of the imprisoned goldsmiths. So he put it in a sack, and carried it to a mill, and said to the miller, "Grind me this sack full of gold into flour." At first the miller stared at him for a madman, but when he saw the letter in Gammelyn's hands which the King had written, and which said, "I'll cut off your head if you don't!", then he set to with a will, and ground the gold into fine golden flour. So Gammelyn shouldered his sack and jogged back to the palace. The next thing he did was to summon all the goldbeaters in the kingdom, which he did easily enough with the King's letter; for directly they saw the words "I'll cut off your head if you don't!" and the King's signature beneath, they came running as fast as their legs could carry them, till all the streets which led up to the palace were full of them.

Then Gammelyn chose a hundred of the strongest, and took them into the chamber where the wedding-dress was in making. And the dress he took and spread out on iron tables, and, sprinkling the golden flour all over it, set the men to beat day and night for a whole week. And at the end of the week there was a splendid dress, that looked as if it were of pure gold only. But the Princess said, "My dress must be *all* gold, and no part cambric—this will not do." "You wait!" said Gammelyn, "it is not finished yet."

Then he made a fire of sweet spices and sandalwood, jasmine, and mignonette; and into the fire he put the wonderful dress.

The Princess screamed with grief and rage; for she was in love with the dress, though she was so nice in holding him to the conditions of the decree. But Gammelyn persevered, and what happened was this: the fire burnt away all the threads of the cambric, but was not hot enough to melt the gold; and when all the cambric was burnt, then he drew out of the fire a dress of beaten gold, light as gossamer, thin as bee's-wing, soft as swan's-down, and fragrant as a wind when it blows through a Sultan's garden.

So all the goldsmiths were set free from prison; and the

King appointed Gammelyn his chief goldsmith.

But when the Princess saw the dress, she was so beside herself with pride and pleasure that she must have also a dress made of pearl, light as gossamer, thin as bee's-wing, soft as swan's-down. And the King sent for all his jewellers, and told them that such a dress was to be made; but they all went down on their bended knees, crying with one voice, "Sire, the thing is not to be done." And all the good they got for that was that they were clapped into prison till a way for doing it should be found.

Then the King said to Gammelyn, "Since my jewellers cannot make this dress, you must do it!" But Gammelyn said, "Sire, that is not in our bargain." And the only answer the King had to that was, "I'll cut off your head if you don't."

Gammelyn sighed like a sea-shell; but determining to make the best of a bad business, he set to work.

And, as before, he made a dress in the fashion the Princess chose, of the finest weaving. He made each part separate; the two sleeves separate, the body separate, the skirt and train separate. Then, at his desire, the King commanded that all the oysters which were dredged out of the sea should be brought to him. Out of these he selected the five finest oysters of all; each one was the size of a tea-tray. Then he put them into a large tank and inside each shell he put one part of the dress—the weaving of which was so fine that there was plenty of room for it, as well as for the oysters. And in course of time he drew out from each shell—from one the body, from one the skirt, from one the train, from one a sleeve, from another the other sleeve. Next he fastened each part together with thread, and put the whole dress back into the tank; and into the mouth of one oyster he put the joinery of body and skirt, and into the mouth of another the joinery of skirt and train, and into the mouth of two others the joinery of the two sleeves, and the fifth oyster he ate. So the oysters did their work, laying their soft inlay over the gown, just as they laid it over the inside of their shells; and after a time Gammelyn drew forth a dress bright and gleaming, and pure mother-o'-pearl. But "No," said the Princess, "it must be all pure pearl, with nothing of thread in it." But, "Wait a while!" said Gammelyn, "I have not finished yet."

So by a decree of the King he caused to be gathered together all the moths in the kingdom—millions of moths; and he put them all into a bare iron room along with the dress, and sealed the doors and windows with red sealing-wax. The Princess wept and sighed for the dress: "It will be all eaten," said she. "Then I shall cut off his head," said the King. But for all that, Gammelyn persevered.

And when he opened the door they found that every thread had been eaten away by the moths, while the mother-o'-pearl had been left uninjured. So the dress was a perfect pearl, light as gossamer, thin as bee's-wing, soft as swan's-down; and the King made Gammelyn his chief jeweller, and set all the other jewellers free.

Then the Princess was so delighted that she wished to have one more dress also, made all of butterflies' wings. "That were easily done," said Gammelyn, "but it were cruel to ask for such a dress to be made."

Nevertheless the Princess would have it so, and *he* should make it. "I'll cut off your head if you don't," said the King.

Gammelyn bumbled like a bee; but all he said was, "Many million butterfles will be wanted for such a work: you must let me have again the two dresses—the pearl, and the gold—for butterflies love bright colours that gleam and shine; and with these alone can I gather them all to one place."

So the Princess gave him the two dresses; and he went to the highest part of the palace, out on to the battlements of the great tower. There he faced towards the west, where lay a new moon, louting towards the setting sun; and he laid the two robes, one on either arm, spreading them abroad till they looked like two wings—a gold and a pearl. And a beam of the sun came and kissed the gold wing, and a pale quivering thread of moonlight touched the pearl wing; and Gammelyn sang:

> "Light of the moon,
> Light of the sun,
> Pearl of the sky,
> Gold from on high,
>   Hearken to me!

> "Light of the moon,
> Pearl of the sea,
> Gold of the land
> Here in my hand,
>   I render to thee.

> "Butterflies come!
> Carry us home,
> Gold of the gnome,
>   Pearl of the sea."

And as he sang, out of the east came a soft muttering of wings and a deep moving mass like a bright storm-cloud. And out of the sun ran a long gold finger, and out of the moon a pale shivering finger of pearl, and touching the gold and the pearl, these became verily wings and not millinery. Then before the Princess could scream more than once, or the King say anything about cutting off heads, the bright cloud in the east became a myriad of butterflies. And drawn by the falling flashing sun, and by the faint falling moon, and fanned by the million wings of his fellow-creatures, Gammelyn sprang out from the palace wall on the crest of the butterfly-wind, and flew away brighter and farther each moment; and followed by his myriad train of butterflies, he passed out of sight, and in that country was never heard of again.

White Birch

NCE upon a time there lived in a wood a brother and sister who had been forgotten by all the world. But this thing did not greatly grieve their hearts, because they themselves were all the world to each other: meeting or parting, they never forgot that. Nobody remained to tell them who they were; but she was "Little Sister," and he was "Fair Brother," and those were the only names they ever went by.

In their little wattled hut they would have been perfectly happy but for one thing which now and then they remembered and grieved over. Fair Brother was lame—not a foot could he put to the ground, nor take one step into the outside world. But he lay quiet on his bed of leaves, while Little Sister went out and in, bringing him food and drink, and the scent of flowers, and tales of the joy of earth and of the songs of birds.

One day she brought him a litter of withered birch-leaves to soften his bed and make it warmer for the approaching season of cold; and all the winter he lay on it, and sighed. Little Sister had never seen him so sad before.

In the spring, when the songs of the pairing birds began, his sorrow only grew greater. "Let me go out, let me go out," he cried; "only a little way into the bright world before I die!" She kissed his feet, and took him up in her arms and carried him. But she could only go a very little way with her burden; presently she had to return and lay him down again on his bed of leaves.

"Have I seen all the bright world?" he asked. "Is it such a little place?"

To hide her sorrow from him, Little Sister ran out into the woods, and as she went, wondering how to comfort his grief, she could not help weeping.

All at once at the foot of a tree she saw the figure of a woman seated. It was strange, for she had never before seen anybody else in the wood but themselves. The woman said to her, "Why is it that you weep so?"

"The heart of Fair Brother is breaking," replied Little Sister. "It is because of that thàt I am weeping."

"Why is his heart breaking?" inquired the other.

"I do not know," answered Little Sister. "Ever since last autumn fell it has been so. Always, before, he has been happy; he has no reason not to be, only he is lame."

She had come close to the seated figure; and looking, she saw a woman with a very white skin, in a robe and hood of deep grey. Grey eyes looked back at her with just a soft touch in them of the green that comes with the young leaves of spring.

"You are beautiful," said Little Sister, drawing in her breath.

"Yes, I am beautiful," answered the other. "Why is Fair Brother lame? Has he no feet?"

"Oh, beautiful feet!" said Little Sister. "But they are like still water; they cannot run."

"If you want him to run," said the other, "I can tell you what to do. What will you give me in exchange?"

"Whatever you like to ask," answered Little Sister; "but I am poor."

"You have beautiful hair," said the woman; "will you let that go?"

Little Sister stooped down her head, and let the other cut

off her hair. The wind went out of it with a sigh as it fell into the grey woman's lap. She hid it away under her robe, and said, "Listen, Little Sister, and I will tell you! Tonight is the new moon. If you can hold your tongue till the moon is full, the feet of Fair Brother shall run like a stream from the hills, dancing from rock to rock."

"Only tell me what I must do!" said Little Sister.

"You see this birch-tree, with its silver skin?" said the woman. "Cut off two strips of it and weave them into shoes for Fair Brother. And when they are finished by the full moon, if you have not spoken, you have but to put them upon Fair Brother's feet, and they will outrun yours."

So Little Sister, as the other had told her, cut off two strips from the bark of the birch-tree, and ran home as fast as she could to tell her brother of the happiness which, with only a little waiting, was in store for them.

But as she came near home, over the low roof she saw the new moon hanging like a white feather in the air; and, closing her lips, she went in and kissed Fair Brother silently.

He said, "Little Sister, loose out your hair over me, and let me feel the sweet airs; and tell me how the earth sounds, for my heart is sick with sorrow and longing." She took his hand and laid it upon her heart that he might feel its happy beating, but said no word. Then she sat down at his feet and began to work at the shoes. All the birch-bark she cut into long strips fit for weaving, doing everything as the grey woman had told her.

Fair Brother fretted at her silence, and cried, calling her cruel; but she only kissed his feet, and went on working the faster. And the white birch shoes grew under her hands; and every night she watched and saw the moon growing round.

Fair Brother said, "Little Sister, what have you done with your hair in which you used to fetch home the wind? And why do you never go and bring me flowers or sing me the song of the birds? And Little Sister looked up and nodded, but never answered or moved from her task, for her fingers were slow, and the moon was quick in its growing.

One night Fair Brother was lying asleep, and his head was filled with dreams of the outer world into which he longed to go. The full moon looked in through the open door, and Little Sister laughed in her heart as she slipped the birch shoes on to his feet. "Now run, dear feet," she whispered; "but do not outrun mine."

Up in his sleep leapt Fair Brother, for the dream of the white birch had hold of him. A lady with a dark hood and grey eyes full of the laughter of leaves beckoned him. Out he ran into the moonlight, and Little Sister laughed as she ran with him.

In a little while she called, "Do not outrun me, Fair Brother!" But he seemed not to hear her, for not a bit did he slacken the speed of his running.

Presently she cried again, "Rest with me a while, Fair Brother! Do not outrun me!" But Fair Brother's feet were fleet after their long idleness, and they only ran the faster. "Ah, ah!" she cried, all out of breath. "Come back to me when you have done running, Fair Brother." And as he disappeared among the trees, she cried after him, "How will you know the way, since you were never here before? Do not get lost in the wood, Fair Brother!"

She lay on the ground and listened, and could hear the white birch shoes carrying him away till all sound of them died.

When, next morning, he had not returned, she searched all day through the wood, calling his name.

"Where are you, Fair Brother? Where have you lost yourself?" she cried, but no voice answered her.

For a while she comforted her heart, saying, "He has not run all these years—no wonder he is still running. When he is tired he will return."

But days and weeks went by, and Fair Brother never came back to her. Every day she wandered searching for him, or sat at the door of the little wattled hut and cried.

One day she cried so much that the ground became quite wet with her tears. That night was the night of the full moon, but weary with grief she lay down and slept soundly, though outside the woods were bright.

In the middle of the night she started up, for she thought she heard somebody go by; and, surely, feet were running away in the distance. And when she looked out, there across the doorway was the print of the birch shoes on the ground she had made wet with her tears.

"Alas, alas!" cried Little Sister. "What have I done that he comes to the very door of our home and passes by, though the moon shines in and shows it him?"

After that she searched everywhere through the forest to discover the print of the birch shoes upon the ground. Here and there after rain she thought she could see traces, but never was she able to track them far.

Once more came the night of the full moon, and once more in the middle of the night Little Sister started up and heard feet running away in the distance. She called, but no answer came back to her.

So on the third full moon she waited, sitting in the door of the hut, and would not sleep.

"If he has been twice," she said to herself, "he will come again, and I shall see him. Ah, Fair Brother, Fair Brother, I have given you feet; why have you so used me?"

Presently she heard a sound of footsteps, and there came Fair Brother running towards her. She saw his face pale and ghostlike, yet he never looked at her, but ran past and on without stopping.

"Fair Brother, Fair Brother, wait for me; do not outrun me!" cried Little Sister; and was up in haste to be after him.

He ran fast, and would not stop; but she ran fast too, for her love would not let him go. Once she nearly had him by the hair, and once she caught him by the cloak; but in her hand it shredded and crumbled like a dry leaf; and still, though there was no breath left in her, she ran on.

And now she began to wonder, for Fair Brother was running the way that she knew well—towards the tree from which she had cut the two strips of bark. Her feet were failing her; she knew that she could run no more. Just as they came together in sight of the birch-tree Little Sister stumbled and fell.

She saw Fair Brother run on and strike with his hands and feet against the tree, and cry, "Oh, White Birch, White Birch, lift the latch up, or she will catch me!" And at once the tree opened its rind, and Fair Brother ran in.

"So," said Little Sister, "you are there, are you, Brother? I know, then, what I have done to you."

She went and laid her ear to the tree, and inside she could hear Fair Brother sobbing and crying. It sounded to her as if White Birch were beating him.

"Well, well, Fair Brother, she shall not beat you for long!" said Little Sister.

She went home and waited till the next full moon had come. Then, as soon as it was dark, she went along through the wood until she came to the place, and there she crept close to the white birch-tree and waited.

Presently she heard Fair Brother's voice come faintly out of the heart of the tree: "White Birch, it is the full moon and the hour in which Little Sister gave life to my feet. For one hour give me leave to go, that I may run home and look at her while she sleeps. I will not stop or speak, and I promise you that I will return."

Then she heard the voice of White Birch answer grudgingly: "It is her hour and I cannot hold you, therefore you may go. Only when you come again I will beat you."

Then the tree opened a little way, and Fair Brother ran out. He ran so quickly in his eager haste that Little Sister had not time to catch him, and she did not dare to call aloud. "I must make sure," she said to herself, "before he comes back. Tonight White Birch will have to let him go."

So she gathered as many dry pieces of wood as she could find, and made them into a pile near at hand; and setting them alight, she soon had a brisk fire burning.

Before long she heard the sound of feet in the brushwood, and there came Fair Brother, running as hard as he could go, with the breath sobbing in and out of his body.

Little Sister sprang out to meet him, but as soon as he saw her he beat with his hands and feet against the tree, crying, "White Birch, White Birch, lift the latch up, or she will catch me!"

But before the tree could open Little Sister had caught hold of the birch shoes, and pulled them off his feet, and running towards the fire she thrust them into the red heart of the embers.

The white birch shivered from head to foot, and broke into lamentable shrieks. The witch thrust her head out of the tree, crying, "Don't, don't! You are burning my skin! Oh, cruel! how you are burning me!"

"I have not burned you enough yet," cried Little Sister; and raking the burning sticks and faggots over the ground, she heaped them round the foot of the white birch-tree, whipping the flames to make them leap high.

The witch drew in her head, but inside she could be heard screaming. As the flames licked the white bark she cried, "Oh, my skin! You are burning my skin. My beautiful white skin will be covered with nothing but blisters. Do you know that you are ruining my complexion?"

But Little Sister said, "If I make you ugly you will not be able to show your face again to deceive the innocent, and to ruin hearts that were happy."

So she piled on sticks and faggots till the outside of the birch-tree was all black and scarred and covered with blisters, the marks of which have remained to this day. And inside, the witch could be heard dancing time to the music of the flames, and crying because of her ruined complexion.

Then Little Sister stooped and took up Fair Brother in her arms. "You cannot walk now," she whispered, "I have taken away your feet; so I will carry you."

He was so starved and thin that he was not very heavy, and all the long way home Little Sister carried him in her arms. How happy they were, looking in each other's eyes by the clear light of the moon!

"Can you ever be happy again in the old way?" asked Little Sister. "Shall you not want to run?"

"No," answered Fair Brother; "I shall never wish to run again. And as for the rest"—he stroked her head softly—"why, I can feel that your hair is growing—it is ever so long, and I can see the wind lifting it. White Birch has no hair of her own, but she has some that she wears, just the same colour as yours."

The Luck of the Roses

OT far from a great town, in the midst of a well-wooded valley, lived a rose-gardener and his wife. All round the old home green sleepy hollows lay girdled by silver streams, long grasses bent softly in the wind, and the half fabulous murmur of woods filled the air.

Up in their rose-garden, on the valley's side facing the sun, the gardener and his wife lived contentedly sharing toil and ease. They had been young, they were not yet old; and though they had to be frugal they did not call themselves poor. A strange fortune had belonged always to the plot of ground over which they laboured; whether because the soil was so rich, or the place so sheltered from cold, or the gardener so skilled in the craft, which had come down in his family from father to son, could not be known; but certainly it was true that his rose-trees gave forth better bloom and bore earlier and later through the season than any others that were to be found in those parts.

The good couple accepted what came to them, simply and gladly, thanking God. Perhaps it was from the kindness of fortune, or perhaps because the sweet perfume of the roses had mixed itself in their blood, that her man and his wife were so sweet-tempered and gentle in their ways. The colour of the rose was in their faces, and the colour of the rose was in their hearts; to her man she was the most beautiful and dearest of sweethearts, to his wife he was the best and kindest of lovers.

Every morning, before it was light, her man and his wife would go into the garden and gather all the roses that were ripe for sale; then with full baskets on their backs they would set out, and get to the market just as the level sunbeams from the east were striking all the vanes and spires of the city into gold. There they would dispose of their flowers to the florists and salesmen of the town, and after that trudge home again to hoe, and dig, and weed, and water, and prune, and plant for the rest of the day. No man ever saw them the one without the other, and the thought that such a thing might some day happen was the only fear and sorrow of their lives.

That they had no children of their own was scarcely a sorrow to them. "It seems to me," said her man after they had been married for some years, "that God means that our roses are to be our children since He has made us love them so much. They will last when we are grown grey, and will support and comfort us in our old age."

All the roses they had were red, and varied little in kind, yet her man and his wife had a name for each of them; to every tree they had given a name, until it almost seemed that the trees knew, and tried to answer when they heard the voices which spoke to them.

"Jane Janet, and you ought to blossom more freely at your age!" his wife might say to one some evening as she went round and watered the flowers; and the next day, when the two came to their dark morning's gathering, Jane Janet would show ten or twelve great blooms under the light of the lantern, every one of them the birth of a single night.

"Mary Maudlin," the gardener would say, as he washed the blight off a favourite rose, "to be sure, you are very beautiful, but did I not love you so, you were more trouble than all your sisters put together." And then all at once great dew-drops would come tumbling down out of Mary Maudlin's

eyes at the tender words of his reproach. So day by day the companionable feet of the happy couple moved to and fro, always intent on the nurture and care of their children.

In their garden they had bees too, who by strange art, unlike other bees, drew all their honey from the roses, and lived in a cone-thatched hive close to the porch; and that honey was famous through all the country-side, for its flavour was like no other honey made in the world.

Sometimes his wife said to her man, "I think our garden is looked after for us by some good Spirit; perhaps it is the Saints after whom we have named our rose-children."

Her man made answer, "It is rich in years, which, like an old wine, have made it gain in flavour; it has been with us from father to son for three hundred years, and that is a great while."

"A full fairy's lifetime!" said his wife. "'Tis a pity we shall not hand it on, being childless."

"When we two die," said her man, "the roses will make us a grave and watch over us." As he spoke a whole shower of petals fell from the trees.

"Did no one pass, just then?" said his wife.

Now one morning, soon after this, in the late season of roses, her man had gone before his wife into the garden, gathering for the market in the grey dusk before dawn; and wherever he went moths and beetles came flocking to the light of his lantern, beating against its horn shutters and crying to get in. Out of each rose, as the light fell on it, winged things sprang up into the darkness; but all the roses were bowed and heavy as if with grief. As he picked them from the stem great showers of dew fell out of them, making pools in the hollow of his palm.

There was such a sound of tears that he stopped to listen; and, surely, from all round the garden came the "drip, drip" of falling dew. Yet the pathways under foot were all dry; there had been no rain and but little dew. Whence was it, then, that the roses so shook and sobbed? For under the stems, surely, there was something that sobbed; and suddenly the light of the lantern took hold of a beautiful small figure, about three feet high, dressed in old rose and green, that went languidly from flower to flower. She lifted up such tired hands to draw their heads down to hers; and to each one she kissed she made a weary little sound of farewell, her beautiful face broken up with grief; and now and then out of her lips ran soft chuckling laughter, as if she still meant to be glad, but could not.

The gardener broke into tears to behold a sight so pitiful; and his wife had stolen out silently to his side, and was weeping too.

"Drip, drip," went the roses: wherever she came and kissed, they all began weeping. The gardener and his wife knelt down and watched her; in and out, in and out, not a rose blossom did she miss. She came nearer and nearer, and at last was standing before them. She seemed hardly able to draw limb after limb, so weak was she; and her filmy garments hung heavy as chains.

A little voice said in their ears, "Kiss me, I am dying!"

They tasted her breath of rose.

"Do not die!" they said simply.

"I have lived three hundred years," she answered. "Now I must die. I am the Luck of the Roses, but I must leave them and die."

"When must you die?" said her man and his wife.

The little lady said: "Before the last roses are over; the chills of night take me, the first frost will kill me. Soon I must die. Now I must dwindle and dwindle, for little life is left to me, and only so can I keep warm. As life and heat grow less, so must I, till presently I am no more."

She was a little thing already—not old, she did not seem old, but delicate as a snowflake, and so weary. She laid her head in the hand of the gardener's wife, and sobbed hard.

"You dear people, who belong so much to me too, I have watched over you."

"Let us watch over you!" said they. They lifted her like a feather-weight, and carried her into the house. There, in the ingle-nook, she sat and shivered, while they brought rose-leaves and piled them round her; but every hour she grew less and less.

Presently the sun shone full upon her from the doorway: its light went through her as through coloured glass; and her man and his wife saw, over the ingle behind her, shadows fluttering as of falling rose-petals: it was the dying rose of her life, falling without end.

All day long she dwindled and grew more weak and frail. Before sunset she was smaller than a small child when it first comes into the world. They set honey before her to taste, but she was too weary to uncurl her tiny hands: they lay like two white petals in the green lap of her gown. The half-filled panniers of roses stood where they had been set down in the porch: the good couple had taken nothing to the market that day. The luck of the house lay dying, for all their care; they could but sit and watch.

When the sun had set, she faded away fast: now she was as small as a young wren. The gardener's wife took her and held her for warmth in the hollow of her hand. Presently she seemed no more than a grasshopper: the tiny chirrup of her voice was heard, about the middle of the night, asking them to take her and lay her among the roses, in the heart of one of the red roses, that there she and death might meet sweetly at the last.

They went together into the dark night, and felt their way among the roses; presently they quite lost her tiny form: she had slipped away into the heart of a Jane Janet rose.

The gardener and his wife went back into the house and sat waiting: they did not know for what, but they were too sad at heart to think just then of sleep.

Soon the first greys of morning began to steal over the world; pale shivers ran across the sky, and one bird chirped in its sleep among the trees.

All at once there rang a soft sound of lamentation among the roses in the rose-garden; again and again, like the cry of many gentle wounded things in pain. The gardener and his wife went and opened the door: they had to tell the bees of the fairy's death. They looked out under the twilight, into the garden they loved. "Drip," "drip," "drip" came the sound of steady weeping under the leaves. Peering out through the shadows they saw all the rose-trees rocking softly for grief.

"Snow?" said his wife to her man.

But it was not snow.

Under the dawn all the roses in the garden had turned white; for they knew that the fairy was dead.

The gardener and his wife woke the bees, and told them of the fairy's death; then they looked in each other's faces, and saw that they, too, had become white and grey.

With gentle eyes the old couple took hands, and went down into the garden to gather white roses for the market.

The Prince with the Nine Sorrows

"Eight white peahens went down to the gate:
    'Wait!' they said, 'little sister, wait!'
They covered her up with feathers so fine;
And none went out, when there went back nine."

 LONG time ago there lived a King and a Queen, who had an only son. As soon as he was born his mother gave him to the forester's wife to be nursed; for she herself had to wear her crown all day and had no time for nursing. The forester's wife had just given birth to a little daughter of her own; but she loved both children equally and nursed them together like twins.

One night the Queen had a dream that made the half of her hair turn grey. She dreamed that she saw the Prince her son at the age of twenty lying dead with a wound over the place of his heart; and near him his foster-sister was standing, with a royal crown on her head, and his heart bleeding between her hands.

The next morning the Queen sent in great haste for the family Fairy, and told her of the dream. The Fairy said, "This can have but one meaning, and it is an evil one. There is some danger that threatens your son's life in his twentieth year, and his foster-sister is to be the cause of it; also, it seems she is to make herself Queen. But leave her to me, and I will avert the evil chance; for the dream coming beforehand shows that the Fates mean that he should be saved."

117

The Queen said, "Do anything; only do not destroy the forester's wife's child, for, as yet at least, she has done no wrong. Let her only be carried away to a safe place and made secure and treated well. I will not have my son's happiness grow out of another one's grave."

The Fairy said, "Nothing is so safe as a grave when the Fates are about. Still, I think I can make everything quite safe within reason, and leave you a clean as well as a quiet conscience."

The little Prince and the forester's daughter grew up together till they were a year old; then, one day, when their nurse came to look for them, the Prince was found, but his foster-sister was lost; and though the search for her was long, she was never seen again, nor could any trace of her be found.

The baby Prince pined and pined, and was so sorrowful over her loss that they feared for a time that he was going to die. But his foster-mother, in spite of her grief over her own child's disappearance, nursed him so well and loved him so much that after a while he recovered his strength.

Then the forester's wife gave birth to another daughter, as if to console herself for the loss of the first. But the same night that the child was born the Queen had just the same dream over again. She dreamed that she saw her son lying dead at the age of twenty; and there was the wound in his breast, and the forester's daughter was standing by with his heart in her hand and a royal crown upon her head.

The poor Queen's hair had gone quite white when she sent again for the family Fairy, and told her how the dream had repeated itself. The Fairy gave her the same advice as before, quieting her fears, and assuring her that however persistent the Fates might be in threatening the Prince's life, all in the end should be well.

Before another year was passed the second of the forester's daughters had disappeared; and the Prince and his foster-mother cried themselves ill over a loss that had been so cruelly renewed. The Queen, seeing how great were the sorrow and the love that the Prince bore for his foster-sisters, began to doubt in her heart and say, "What have I done? Have I saved my son's life by taking away his heart?"

Now every year the same thing took place, the forester's wife giving birth to a daughter, and the Queen on the same night having the same fearful dream of the fate that threatened her son in his twentieth year; and afterwards the family Fairy would come, and then one day the forester's wife's child would disappear, and be heard of no more.

At last when nine daughters in all had been born to the forester's wife and lost to her when they were but a year old, the Queen fell very ill. Every day she grew weaker and weaker, and the little Prince came and sat by her, holding her hand and looking at her with a sorrowful face. At last one night (it was just a year after the last of the forester's children had disappeared) she woke suddenly, stretching out her arms and crying. "Oh, Fairy," she cried, "the dream, the dream!" And covering her face with her hands, she died.

The little Prince was now more than ten years old, and the very saddest of mortals. He said that there were nine sorrows hidden in his heart, of which he could not get rid; and that at night, when all the birds went home to roost, he heard cries of lamentation and pain; but whether these came from very far away, or out of his own heart he could not tell.

Yet he grew slenderly and well, and had such grace and tenderness in his nature that all who saw him loved him. His foster-mother, when he spoke to her of his nine sorrows, tried to comfort him, calling him her own nine joys; and, indeed, he was all the joy left in life for her.

When the Prince neared his twentieth year, the King his father felt that he himself was becoming old and weary of life. "I shall not live much longer," he thought: "very soon my son will be left alone in the world. It is right, therefore, now that he should know of the danger ahead that threatens his life." For till then the Prince had not known anything; all had been kept a secret between the Queen and the King and the family Fairy.

The old King knew of the Prince's nine sorrows, and often he tried to believe that they came by chance, and had nothing to do with the secret that sat at the root of his son's life. But now he feared more and more to tell the Prince the story of those nine dreams, lest the knowledge should indeed serve but as the crowning point of his sorrows, and altogether break his heart for him.

Yet there was so much danger in leaving the thing untold that at last he summoned the Prince to his bedside, meaning to tell him all. The King had worn himself so ill with anxiety and grief in thinking over the matter, that now to tell all was the only means of saving his life.

The Prince came and knelt down, and leaned his head on his father's pillow; and the King whispered into his ear the story of the dreams, and of how for his sake all the Prince's foster-sisters had been spirited away.

Before his tale was done he could no longer bear to look into his son's face, but closed his eyes, and, with long silences between, spoke as one who prayed.

When he had ended he lay quite still, and the Prince kissed his closed eyelids and went softly out of the room.

"Now I know," he said to himself; "now at last!" And he came through the wood and knocked at his foster-mother's door. "Other mother," he said to her, "give me a kiss for each of my sisters, for now I am going out into the world to find them, to be rid of the sorrows in my heart."

"They can never be found!" she cried, but she kissed him nine times. "And this," she said, "was Monica, and this was Ponica, and this was Veronica," and she went over every name. "But now they are only names!" she wept, as she let him go.

He went along, and he went along, mile after mile. "Where may you be going to, fair sir?" asked an old peasant, at whose cabin the Prince sought shelter when night came to the first day of his wanderings. "Truly," answered the Prince, "I do not know how far or whither I need to go; but I have a finger-post in my heart that keeps pointing me."

So that night he stayed there, and the next day he went on.

"Where to so fast?" asked a woodcutter when the second night found him in the thickest and loneliest parts of the forest. "Here the night is so dark and the way so dangerous, one like you should not go alone."

"Nay, I know nothing," said the Prince, "only I feel like a weather-cock in a wind that keeps turning me to its will!"

After many days he came to a small long valley rich in woods and water-courses, but no road ran through it. More and more it seemed like the world's end, a place unknown, or forgotten of its old inhabitants. Just at the end of the valley, where the woods opened into clear slopes and hollows towards the west, he saw before him, low and overgrown, the walls of a little tumble-down grange. "There," he said to himself when he saw it, "I can find shelter for tonight. Never have I felt so tired before, or such a pain at my heart!"

Before long he came to a little gate, and a winding path that led in among lawns and trees to the door of an old house. The house seemed as if it had been once lived in, but there was no sign of any life about it now. He pushed open the door, and suddenly there was a sharp rustling of feathers, and nine white peahens rose up from the ground and flew out of the window into the garden.

The Prince searched the whole house over, and found it a mere ruin; the only signs of life to be seen were the white feathers that lifted and blew about over the floors.

Outside, the garden was gathering itself together in the dusk, and the peahens were stepping daintily about the lawns, picking here and there between the blades of grass. They seemed to suit the gentle sadness of the place, which had an air of grief that has grown at ease with itself.

The Prince went out into the garden, and walked about among the quietly stepping birds; but they took no heed of him. They came picking up their food between his very feet, as though he were not there. Silence held all the air, and in the cleft of the valley the day drooped to its end.

Just before it grew dark, the nine white peahens gathered together at the foot of a great elm, and lifting up their throats they wailed in chorus. Their lamentable cry touched the Prince's heart; "Where," he asked himself, "have I heard such sorrow before?" Then all with one accord the birds sprang rustling up to the lowest boughs of the elm, and settled themselves to roost.

The Prince went back to the house, to find some corner amid its half-ruined rooms to sleep in. But there the air was close, and an unpleasant smell of moisture came from the floor and walls: so, the night being warm, he returned to the garden, and folding himself in his cloak lay down under the tree where the nine peahens were at roost.

For a long time he tried to sleep, but could not, there was so much pain and sorrow in his heart.

Presently when it was close upon midnight, over his head one of the birds stirred and ruffled through all its feathers; and he heard a soft voice say:

"Sisters, are you awake?"

All the other peahens lifted their heads, and turned towards the one that had spoken, saying, "Yes, sister, we are awake."

Then the first one said again, "Our brother is here."

They all said, "He is our enemy; it is for him that we endure this sorrow."

"Tonight," said the first, "we may all be free."

They answered, "Yes, we may all be free! Who will go down and peck out his heart? Then we shall be free."

And the first who had spoken said, "I will go down!"

"Do not fail, sister!" said all the others. "For if you fail you can speak to us no more."

The first peahen answered, "Do not fear that I shall fail!" And she began stepping down the long boughs of the elm.

The Prince lying below heard all that was said. "Ah! poor sisters," he thought, "have I found you at last; and are all these sorrows brought upon you for me?" And he unloosed his doublet, and opened his vest, making his breast bare for the peahen to come and peck out his heart.

He lay quite still with his eyes shut, and when she reached the ground the peahen found him lying there, as it seemed to her fast asleep, with his white breast bare for the stroke of her beak.

Then so fair he looked to her, and so gentle in his youth, that she had pity on him, and stood weeping by his side, and laying her head against his, whispered, "O, brother, once we lay as babes together and were nursed at the same breast! How can I peck out your heart?"

Then she stole softly back into the tree, and crouched down again by her companions. They said to her, "Our minute of midnight is nearly gone. Is there blood on your beak! Have you our brother's heart for us?" But the other answered never a word.

In the morning the peahens came rustling down out of

the elm, and went searching for fat carnation buds and anemone seeds among the flower-beds in the garden. To the Prince they showed no sign either of hatred or fear, but went to and fro carelessly, pecking at the ground about his feet. Only one came with drooping head and wings, and sleeked itself to his caress, and the Prince, stooping down, whispered in her ear, "O, sister, why did you not peck out my heart?"

At night, as before, the peahens all cried in chorus as they went up into the elm; and the Prince came and wrapped himself in his cloak, and lay down at the foot of it to watch.

At midnight the eight peahens lifted their heads, and said, "Sister, why did you fail last night?" But their sister gave them not a word.

"Alas!" they said, "now she has failed, unless one of us succeed, we shall never hear her speak with her human voice again. Why is it that you weep so," they said again, "now when deliverance is so near?" For the poor peahen was shaken with weeping, and her tears fell down in loud drops upon the ground.

Then the next sister said, "I will go down! He is asleep. Be certain, I will not fail!" So she climbed softly down the tree, and the Prince opened his shirt and laid his breast bare for her to come and take out his heart.

Presently she stood by his side, and when she saw him, she too had pity on him for the youth and kindness of his face. And at once she shut her eyes, and lifted her head for the stroke; but then weakness seized her, and she laid her head softly upon his heart and said, "Once the breast that gave me milk gave milk also to you. You were my sister's brother, and she spared you. How can I peck out your heart?" And having said this she went softly back into the tree, and crouched down again among her sisters.

They said to her, "Have you blood upon your beak? Is

his heart ours?" But she answered them no word.

The next day the two sisters, who because their hearts betrayed them had become mute, followed the Prince wherever he went, and stretched up their heads to his caress. But the others went and came indifferently, careless except for food; for until midnight their human hearts were asleep; only now the two sisters who had given their voices away had regained their human hearts perpetually.

That night the same thing happened as before. "Sisters," said the youngest, "tonight I will go down, since the two eldest of us have failed. My wrong is fresher in my heart than theirs! Be sure I shall not fail!" So the youngest peahen came down from the tree, and the Prince laid his heart bare for her beak; but the bird could not find the will to peck it out. And so it was the next night, and the next, until eight nights were gone.

So at last only one peahen was left. At midnight she raised her head, saying, "Sisters, are you awake?"

They all turned, and gazed at her weeping, but could say no word.

Then she said, "You have all failed, having all tried but me. Now if I fail we shall remain mute and captive for ever, more undone by the loss of our last remaining gift of speech than we were at first. But I tell you, dear sisters, I will not fail; for the happiness of you all lies with me now!"

Then she went softly down the tree; and one by one they all went following her, and weeping, to see what the end would be.

They stood some way apart, watching with upturned heads, and their poor throats began catching back a wish to cry as the little peahen, the last of the sisters, came and stood by the Prince.

Then she, too, looked in his face, and saw the white breast made bare for her beak; and the love of him went deep down into her heart. And she tried and tried to shut her eyes and deal the stroke, but could not.

She trembled and sighed, and turned to look at her sisters, where they all stood weeping silently together. "They have spared him," she said to herself: "why should not I?"

But the Prince, seeing that she, too, was about to fail like the rest of them, turned and said, as if in his sleep, "Come, come, little peahen, and peck out my heart!"

At that she turned back again to him, and laid her head down upon his heart and cried more sadly than them all.

Then he said, "You have eight sisters, and a mother who cries for her children to return!" Yet still she thought he was dreaming, and speaking only in his sleep. The other peahens came no nearer, but stood weeping silently. She looked from him to them. "O," she cried, "I have a wicked heart, to let one stand in the way of nine!" Then she threw up her neck and cried lamentably with her peafowl's voice, wishing that the Prince would wake up and see her, and so escape. And at that all the other peahens lifted up their heads and wailed with her: but the Prince never turned, nor lifted a finger, nor uttered a sound.

Then she drew in a deep breath, and closed her eyes fast. "Let my sisters go, but let me be as I am!" she cried; and with that she stooped down, and pecked out his heart.

All her sisters shrieked as their human shapes returned to them. "Oh, sister! O, wicked little sister!" they cried, "What have you done?"

The little white peahen crouched close down to the side of the dead Prince. "I loved him more than you all!" she tried to say: but she only lifted her head, and wailed again and again the peafowl's cry.

The Prince's heart lay beating at her feet, so glad to be rid of its nine sorrows that mere joy made it live on, though all the rest of the body lay cold.

The peahen leaned down upon the Prince's breast, and there wailed without ceasing: then suddenly, piercing with her beak her own breast, she drew out her own living heart and laid it in the place where his had been.

And, as she did so, the wound where she had pierced him closed and became healed; and her heart was, as it were, buried in the Prince's breast. In her death agony she could feel it there, her own heart leaping within his breast for joy.

The Prince, who had seemed to be dead, flushed from head to foot as the warmth of life came back to him; with one deep breath he woke, and found the little white peahen lying as if dead between his arms.

Then he laughed softly and rose (his goodness making him wise), and taking up his own still beating heart he laid it into the place of hers. At the first beat of it within her breast, the peahen became transformed as all her sisters had been, and her own human form came back to her. And the pain and the wound in her breast grew healed together, so that she stood up alive and well in the Prince's arms.

"Dear heart!" said he: and "Dear, dear heart!" said she; but whether they were speaking of their own hearts or of each other's, who can tell? for which was which they themselves did not know.

Then all round was so much embracing and happiness that it is out of reach for tongue or pen to describe. For truly the Prince and his foster-sisters loved each other well, and could put no bounds upon their present contentment. As for the Prince and the one who had plucked out his heart, of no two was the saying ever more truly told that they had lost their hearts to each other; nor was ever love in the world known before that carried with it such harmony as theirs.

And so it all came about according to the Queen's dream,

that the forester's daughter wore the royal crown upon her head, and held the Prince's heart in her hand.

Long before he died the old King was made happy because the dream he had so much feared had become true. And the forester's wife was happy before she died. And as for the Prince and his wife and his foster-sisters, they were all rather happy; and none of them is dead yet.